We lucked out. Denise hurried across the wooden pier ahead of us and let out a squeal. She pointed with her feather at the parking lot below. Two men stood next to the green Thunderbird. I had never seen the lunky one with the bumpy complexion before. But I recognized the tall, thin man in the flowered Hawaiian shirt. It was Evil Eyes.

"Get down," Wil ordered in a low voice. "And keep quiet." After dropping onto our stomachs, we inched toward the edge of the wooden pier until we could peek over. It was the perfect place to spy. From below, the words of the two men drifted up.

"Message just came . . . ship-to-shore radio," Evil Eyes said. "The boat's due on Friday . . . about twelve."

"How many birds?" the lunky man asked.

"Dunno . . . Transmission was garbled—"

"*Oops!*" Denise shrieked as her feather floated down toward the men. Evil Eyes spun around.

"*Who's up there?*" he demanded, shaking his fist. . . .

THE
PARROT
MAN
MYSTERY

Kathy Pelta

FAWCETT JUNIPER • NEW YORK

Contents

1	Nothing but Trouble	1
2	A Big Mistake	9
3	The Sheriff Arrives	18
4	A Secret and a Clue	26
5	A Mysterious Phone Call	37
6	A Startling Discovery	41
7	The Letter from Brazil	46
8	On the Trail of Evil Eyes	50
9	Spies on the Pier	57
10	The Promise	66
11	The Message in the Margin	74
12	A Crisis!	79
13	Caught in the Act	85
14	A Secret Visitor	90
15	Where Is WB?	93
16	The Zero Hour	97
17	Lookout for Smugglers	102
18	Trapped!	107
19	A Prisoner	110
20	Contraband	114
21	Two Mysteries Solved	118

With thanks to Bill Dusel
of the U.S. Fish and Wildlife Service
for his help and encouragement
—K.P.

1

Nothing but Trouble

I RACED INTO THE PET SHOP.

"Mr. Willy-Bones! I need puppy biscuits for Hilda." I slammed a quarter on the counter. "As many as this will buy."

The old shopkeeper was at his bulletin board, tacking up a notice. I was too far away to read all of it. But I couldn't miss the two words in big letters at the top: BIRD SMUGGLERS!

"What's *that* about?" I asked.

"Bad guys," he said.

"You mean *here*? In Pacific Cliffs?"

"Yah, could be," he said, his double chins wobbling. "Up the coast by Malibu."

I knew about the smugglers in Texas who stole my aunt's necklace. I even helped catch them. But I knew *nothing* about bird smugglers from around here. I hoped they wouldn't make off with Mr. Willy-Bones's valuable birds—*especially* Ringo, the parakeet I wanted to buy.

As the shopkeeper dropped the puppy biscuits into a paper bag one by one, he counted to himself in Swedish—*"ett, tva, tre, fyra."* It didn't look like twenty-five cents' worth. But then Mr. Willy-Bones gave me a wink and slipped one more in the bag.

"Five!" he said—in English this time. Only, with his accent it sounded like "Fife!"

Grabbing the bag, I dashed for the door. No time to find out about the smugglers now. I was pet-sitting and had to rescue Hilda, Mrs. Eastley's dachshund, from the next-door neighbor. As far as I was concerned, that nasty man and his mean-tempered parrot were the *real* bad guys. Not some parrot smugglers—who probably didn't even exist! If Hilda left the house and wandered into that Parrot Man's yard . . . it could be the end of her. I shuddered at the thought and ran the entire ten blocks to Mrs. Eastley's.

Fortunately all was quiet when I got there. No sounds came from the other side of the hedge, where the Parrot Man lived. Then I heard Hilda's bark, from Mrs. Eastley's kitchen.

"Hilda?" I called. The flap of the doggy door moved, and the little sausage dog waddled out. She wiggled and yipped as I petted her. I gave her one puppy biscuit.

"More later," I promised. "After your walk."

I snapped the leather leash to her collar, and we started across the yard. Suddenly a voice squawked, "Bad dog!"

The words came from somewhere high up the thorny hedge. When Hilda began to yip, the scolding grew sharper.

"*Bad dog!* Bad. Bad. BAD!"

Hilda barked even louder. She strained at the leash. I held tight. Would the old dog attack the voice or run from it? Then Hilda lunged. I tried to hold her back, but a ninety-pound, eleven-and-a-half-year-old girl like me was no match for a ten-pound, aging but determined dachshund.

Near the top of the hedge flashed a fan of red feathers.

"Hilda!" I screamed. "Come away."

But the dog froze. A red parrot bore down on her like a jet fighter. Its huge beak cut through Hilda's leash. Two inches closer and it would have slashed the dachshund's neck. Screeching and snapping, the bird circled for another attack.

I swung my pack to fend it off. "Leave Hilda alone!"

With a shriek the parrot vanished into the top of the hedge. Hilda staggered under the hedge and crouched, trembling.

The day Mrs. Eastley hired me to look after Hilda, she warned me about the man next door. "Stay clear of that trouble-maker," she'd said. "And don't ever tangle with that nasty-tempered bird of his." She wasn't kidding.

I grabbed for Hilda. She acted scared and confused, and scrambled farther back.

"Not *that* way!" I yelled. "That's where the parrot lives."

Too late! Already Hilda had vanished into the yard next door.

Drat! That parrot could turn the sausage dog into *real* sausage. Dropping pack and leash, I tore across Mrs. Eastley's front lawn to the street. But when I came to her neighbor's yard, my steps slowed.

That man with the parrot had the only yard on this side of the street with a chain-link fence. Not very friendly! And ivy grew so thickly over the fence that I couldn't see in. Worse than unfriendly—it was scary!

At the gate I stopped. Plastic strips were woven through the gate's steel links. I couldn't see in. What was that Parrot Man hiding in his yard? I like playing detective, but being here didn't seem like such a good idea after all.

As I backed away, a white Mercedes splashed through a puddle, spattering mud on my white shorts and purple T-shirt. Dumb driver!

I glared after the sports car, then once more faced the Parrot Man's gate.

"Bad!" Now the squawk came from behind the fence.

I paused, remembering Mrs. Eastley's warning about the parrot's temper. Instead of barging in, maybe I should wait for Hilda to come home on her own.

But what if she didn't? What if I was too late already?

My mind was a jumble. Should I go into the Parrot Man's yard, or retreat? Hilda's frightened yip made the decision for me. I couldn't let that dog become parrot chow.

Taking a deep breath, I opened the gate and stepped inside. The yips and squawks ceased. I looked around the dusty yard. No Hilda, no parrot, but cracked flowerpots and rusting tools lay everywhere. The yard seemed messy, not sinister. Was that the man's secret: He was a junk dealer?

"Hilda? Where are you?" I peeked under a faded sofa. It was missing two legs and most of its stuffing. Hilda wasn't there, nor was she behind the splintered wooden crates stacked against the fence.

In a vegetable garden a spindly scarecrow stood guard. Its black hat flapped in the sea breeze. But no dog crouched among the beans and tomato plants. Suddenly from behind me came a loud squawk and Hilda's frantic yips. I whirled around.

Was she in the Parrot Man's cottage? Thick vines and tropical plants hid the porch from view. Maybe the yard was only junky, but the house was sinister. It gave me the creeps. From a safe distance I called, "Hilda? Are you in there?"

The dog tore around the corner of the cottage, chased by a man in baggy red swim trunks and a white T-shirt. On his shoulder rode the parrot.

"No-good mutt!" the man yelled at Hilda. "Get outa here!"

"Outa here! Outa here!" echoed the parrot.

As fast as her stiff hind legs would allow, Hilda streaked

past me into the garden. She began circling the scarecrow. The man gained on her, his stringy gray ponytail flapping in the wind. He snatched up a garden hoe.

"No!" I cried.

The man spun around.

"Don't hit her!" I raced over to grab Hilda.

The man threw down the hoe. "I told that old witch . . ." He waved a skinny arm toward the hedge separating his yard from Mrs. Eastley's. "I told her if her mutt came in my garden again I'd call the authorities. And by Jupiter, I will. I mean it."

"Mean it! Mean it!" screamed the parrot.

"Please," I begged. "Don't call the police. It wasn't Hilda's fault. When Mrs. Eastley's gone, she gets nervous—"

"And my Casper gets nervous when that mutt's around, so we're even." His bony fingers stroked the bird's bright feathers. Then he scowled at Hilda. "Now get that pest outa my yard. *Scoot.*"

I grabbed Hilda and dashed out the gate, not stopping until I sank, gasping for breath, on Mrs. Eastley's back step. Hilda whimpered. Her heart still thumped wildly.

"Don't have a heart attack, Hilda. How would I ever explain it to Mrs. Eastley?"

While soothing the trembling dog, I kept glancing at the hedge. But no red macaw lurked, ready to pounce. For a long time I stayed with Hilda. Though I now had a half dozen clients to care for, she was my first. I felt loyal to the little wiener dog.

"That was a close call," I said, stroking her velvety ears. The soft fur reminded me of the many pet hamsters I'd had in my life. "If I lost you, Hilda, my reputation as a pet-sitter would fizzle. Nobody in town would hire me. I'd *never* earn enough money to buy Ringo."

Ringo was the beautiful green-and-yellow parakeet at

Mr. Willy-Bones's pet shop. I started my pet-sitting service to save enough money to buy him. Of course, I liked all kinds of pets. I wouldn't be in this business if I didn't. But I wanted a pet that could talk. Ringo wasn't like that mean red parrot, though. Ringo was a gentle bird.

The morning sun was high in the sky. "Have to go," I said, putting Hilda down. She whined to be held. "Sorry, old girl. Other clients are waiting. Also, I have to buy you a new leash."

I unhooked the stub of strap at her collar and dropped both parts of the leash in my pack. "To know what size to buy," I explained.

Too bad! A real leather leash would use up more than a week's pet-sitting profits. But Mrs. Eastley would be sure to notice if I got cheap plastic. I'd have to pay with my savings, too. All the money she'd left me was a few quarters to buy puppy biscuits. Then I had an awful thought. What if she didn't pay me back?

I jumped up. "Hilda, I need more customers. And from now on, they have to pay in advance. And I won't ask a quarter a day. I'm charging a dollar."

I gave the old dog a nudge. "Time to go in."

She waddled across the porch, her old nails scratching the wooden floor and her sagging tummy nearly scraping bottom. At her doggy door she stopped. Lifting the flap, I urged her in.

"It's okay, Hilda. You'll be safe in your very own kitchen."

I pushed two puppy biscuits in after her, then left.

Passing the Parrot Man's ivy-covered fence, I got mad all over again. It wasn't fair that *I* had to buy that leash. The parrot had trashed it. Its owner should pay. I ought to tell him so. In fact, I would—right now! Before my mind could flip-flop, I flung open the gate and charged in.

"Hello?"

No answer. I walked across the man's trashy yard. Then I spotted him, the bird on his shoulder. He stood on the roof of a shed by the back fence, waving two red flags. It looked like he was signaling somebody on the beach or in a boat. Strange! I moved closer.

"Sir?"

At my shout the flags clattered on the roof, and the man spun around. "What're *you* doing back here?"

I showed him the cut leash. "Your parrot did this."

"Eh?" He cupped a gnarled hand to his ear. "Speak up."

"Your parrot did this."

"No need to bellow." The wiry old man hopped down the rungs of a ladder. I noticed the telescope mounted on the shed's flat roof. What was this guy up to?

"Since your bird cut up Hilda's leash . . ."

The parrot's sharp talons gripped the man's shoulder. With unblinking eyes it stared at me. I stepped back.

"I just think . . ." I went on ". . . you should . . . buy a new one."

Taking one of the pieces of leather, he rubbed it between thumb and forefinger. "Mighty thin." He tossed it back. "Musta been wore out already."

My jaw fell. Wasn't he going to do anything about it? "The strap was fine till your bird bit it. I was walking Hilda—"

"Eh?"

"*Hilda.* Mrs. Eastley's dog," I yelled. "You see, I have this pet-sitting business, and—"

"What kind of business?" The man's eyes narrowed.

"I sit pets."

I handed him one of Mom's cards. I'd drawn a line through her name and title, "Ellen Kincaid, Commercial Pilot," and over them I'd written, "M.D.K., Pet Specialist."

"What's *that* s'posed to mean—'Mighty Dumb Kid'?"

"They're my initials." I glared at him. "My name's Margaret Drusilla Kincaid."

"Humph." He gave back the card. "Got a permit? Need a permit to run a business."

When I shook my head, he waved an arm. "Scram!" he snapped. "I'm busy."

"But . . . but . . ."

"Go away—before I call the authorities."

Would he really do that, and ruin my business? As I backed off, I looked at him. Was that a wink beneath those bushy gray eyebrows? No way! Not from that grouch. He was just squinting at the bright sun. Suddenly the parrot sprang from his shoulder.

"Away!" it screeched, driving at me. *"Go away!"*

I ran!

2

A Big Mistake

ONCE ACROSS THE STREET I FELT SAFE. I SANK TO the ground, gasping for breath. The parrot's screeching had stopped. Over the thudding of my heart in my ears there was only the far-off sound of waves slapping the beach. It was soothing. After a while my heart no longer felt like it would jump from my chest.

I looked at the blue Pacific. The sky was so clear, you could almost see Hawaii. For sure I could see up the coast to Malibu. . . .

Malibu! I jumped up. That's where the smugglers were. I wished I knew more about them. Maybe their hideout was in those cliffs near Malibu Beach. When I went back to the pet shop, I'd ask Mr. Willy-Bones.

Now, though, I had to get going. Darn that Parrot Man! He made me waste half my morning. I'd be lucky to finish my rounds by five—with hardly any time left to look for new clients.

Grabbing my pack, I started down Edgecliff Road. A silver Rolls-Royce glided by. It paused at the entrance to Edgecliff Estates, and then the guard waved it through.

That gave me an idea!

Why not detour through the Estates? I could look for new customers now. It wouldn't take long. And with just a few rich clients from here, my money worries would be over.

I hurried to the entrance. Putting on what I hoped was a convincing smile, I strode up to the guard. He wasn't fooled. He knew I didn't live here.

"Hold it, young lady." He eyed the mud spots on my clothes. "Visiting somebody?"

I nodded. "A friend."

"Name?"

"The name of my friend, you mean?" I tried to think. Did anyone in my sixth-grade class live here?

"Well, she's not really a friend." I was stalling for time. "She's more like an acquaintance." My mind was a blank. All I could think of were my friends from the east side of town.

A Mercedes 350SL slammed to a stop—the same car that had splashed mud on me. The guard waved him by. The driver was Floyd Barker, host of *Uncle Floyd's Kiddie Brigade* on TV—and also Denise Barker's stepdad! What luck! I'd forgotten about Denise. She'd skipped a year, so she was younger than the rest of our class. And smarter, too! But we *did* know each other. And she lived in the Estates!

I grinned at the guard. "Denise Barker," I said. "That's who I'm visiting."

With a grunt he motioned me through.

I'd never been to Denise's house. Maybe she wasn't even home. Who cared? I was here! Now to find a movie star or rich banker walking a poodle with a diamond-studded collar. But after circling three blocks, I met no one. This detour was a mistake. Then something soft rubbed my ankle. I heard a faint meow. It was tabby—but too skinny to be an Estates "fat cat."

As I stooped to pet it, someone called, "Margaret!"

The cat skittered up a tree, and I looked around. Denise

was waving at me from the yard of a huge, Spanish-style house next door. "What brings you here?" she asked.

"Looking for customers. For my pet-sitting service." I pointed to the tabby in the oak tree. "Is it yours?"

Denise shook her head. "I *yearn* for a cat. But Floyd *refuses* to permit one in the house." She wrinkled her nose. "Allergic!"

Then she smiled and fluffed her shiny black bangs. "Describe your service. Is it fun?"

"If you can call getting attacked by a parrot fun."

"You must be referring to that scarlet macaw." She nodded. "A real menace! Its wings ought to be clipped. It perches on the shoulder of an ancient bicyclist who rides past here sometimes. A very peculiar individual."

"Mean, too." I was wondering how the Parrot Man sneaked past the gatekeeper.

I reached into my pack. "Here," I said, handing Denise one of my cards. "In case you hear of someone needing a pet-sitter."

Wrinkling her nose again, Denise studied the card. " 'M.D.K.'?"

"My new nickname. From when I was visiting in Texas."

She smiled. "I read the newspaper account of your exploits. A detective enterprise would seem more appropriate, considering how brilliantly you outwitted those criminal types."

I groaned. "Dictionary Denise" was at it again! "Tracked the smugglers, you mean? Pets seem a more sure way to make money," I said. "Except not lately. . . ."

"Obviously your business needs a motto." She cocked her head. "How about, 'Sit Your Pet? You Bet!'?"

I grinned. "It might help. I'll try it. Thanks."

Denise twisted a strand of hair. "What varieties of pets do you sit?"

"All kinds. Birds. Raccoons. Rabbits. Cats—"

Her black eyes lit up. "I have always *longed* for a cat."

"Not Conrad. No claws—but he bites."

"Undoubtedly lonesome," she said. "He craves attention. Do you play with him?"

"No time. I'm too busy with—"

"Let me," she broke in. "I would love to take care of Conrad for you. I *adore* felines."

Suddenly I had an idea—a way to finish today's rounds in a hurry, and find the new clients I needed besides.

"Want to be my partner for the day?" I asked.

"Hmm." She wrinkled her nose. "All right. It might be fun."

I grabbed her hand. "It's a deal."

Denise nodded solemnly. "I must tell Floyd." She slipped past the Mercedes parked in the drive and ducked into the house.

When she came out again, she carried a tennis racket. Floyd stormed behind her. His frown vanished when he saw me. He brushed thin wisps of hair over his bald spot, as if the TV cameras were about to roll, and flashed a big smile, his gleaming teeth matching his white patent-leather shoes.

That phony grin didn't fool me.

He got in his car. With a squeal of tires he blasted off.

"Where's he headed in such a hurry?" I asked.

"To our beach house." Denise rolled her eyes. "Preparations for yet *another* stupendous fishing trip." Grinning, she tossed the tennis racket into a geranium patch. "I had to tell him we were playing tennis so he would let me join you today."

"Where's your mom?" I asked as we started down the drive.

She shrugged. "At the country club. Losing, as usual."

"Losing what?"

"At bridge."

With Denise to help, I breezed through my rounds. And it was fun having someone to yak with, even if she did use lots of big words. We talked about my pet clients. In school Denise acted like she was too much of a brain to mix with the rest of us. She kept to herself. Now she wasn't stuck-up—though she still talked like an encyclopedia with legs.

But that was a good thing. Denise knew a lot about bird smugglers! She told me that they bring birds *into* the United States—not take them out. What a relief! Ringo wouldn't get whisked away after all.

Denise said that in order to sneak past the border guards, smugglers stuff baby parrots into nylon panty hose and hide them under the floorboards of cars or in spare tires. It sounded awful.

"Countless birds suffocate," she said, "before they ever get here."

I felt sick. "How could *anybody* do that to a baby bird?"

"Money," said Denise. "Those rare parrots are worth a fortune. People will pay thousands of dollars for one. Although I fail to understand why *anyone* would want a talking bird."

"I do," I said, and I told her about Ringo. "He's the reason for my pet-sitting business. I need money fast."

"Why such haste? Is he about to fly off?"

"Not fly off. Get sold. If anyone wants him, Mr. Willy-Bones will have to let Ringo go—unless I can come up with the money."

"Bones?" She squinted. "What kind of bones?"

I laughed. "He's the pet-shop owner. He's from Sweden, and his name is Wilhelm Bjornson. It's hard to say, so he lets us kids call him Willy-Bones."

"So how expensive *is* your parakeet?" Denise asked.

"Seventy-five dollars."

"Excessive!" Again she rolled her eyes. "That much, for an ordinary bird?"

"Ringo is a rare Indian ringneck. Wait'll you see. So far I've saved thirty-two dollars." I bit my lip. "I still need forty-three more."

Maybe to a rich kid like Denise it didn't sound like much. But all she said was, "I prefer cats. You can play with cats."

"Only they can't talk." I laughed. "But I have to get Ringo away from the pet shop soon or he'll have a Swedish accent."

"Floyd once owned a cockatoo that said 'Buenos días.' "

"What else did you teach it?"

"Me?" Denise looked disgusted. "Floyd would never allow *me* near his precious birds. Not that I minded. Soon he got bored with birds anyway," she went on. "So he purchased tropical fish. He tired of those and bought a boat. Now he is into deep-sea fishing in Mexico."

"Does he go often?"

"Not often enough. I wish he would go down and *stay*."

The way she said it, I almost felt sorry for her. At least I missed my folks when they were away.

We worked so fast that by one o'clock we were down to my last two clients—Puddy Kenilworth's goldfish and Kim's tortoise. Denise had even had time to play with Conrad, the clawless cat, who didn't try once to bite her.

We went to Kim's first, where her tortoise was sunning on the back patio. He didn't look up when I shook the lettuce and apple pieces into his food pan. He didn't even peek out when Denise tapped his shell.

"Ugh!" Denise rolled her eyes once again. "I should have stayed with Conrad. . . . Let us go feed the fish."

"Let's save feeding the fish until after lunch," I said.

"I'm starved. And Puddy lives on the steepest hill in Pacific Cliffs."

"Good," said Denise. "I despise hills. Only—I brought nothing to eat."

"That's okay. Have a peanut-butter sandwich. Shirlee made three."

Denise took it and nodded thanks. "Who is Shirlee?"

"A friend of my mom's from Texas. She's sitting while my folks are gone. Mom is flying charter for some politician," I explained. "And Dad went to Oklahoma on a business trip."

Denise bit into the sandwich and made a face.

"A decided and *unmistakable* taste of chili."

I nodded. "You get used to it. Chili is Shirlee's specialty. She cooks *gallons*. More than we can ever eat. And it seems to get into everything she fixes."

"What does she do with so much chili?"

"Good question. I'm not sure."

Denise took another bite. "I shall *definitely* bring tuna fish tomorrow."

It sounded like we were partners for more than just today. I was glad. She'd be a real help. She had been this morning. Now we'd have the whole afternoon to find new clients.

As we climbed the hill to Puddy's house, Denise stopped to catch her breath. "I have a brilliant suggestion. If you feed the fish by yourself tomorrow, I will walk that dachshund for you."

"That *is* brilliant! Getting over to Hilda early enough is really hard," I said. "I live so far away."

"It is no problem for me," she said. "I live very close." She pushed her bangs back from her sweaty forehead. "Anyway, to avoid this agonizing climb, I would do *anything*."

As soon as we got to the garage where Puddy kept his

fish, Denise rushed to the laundry sink. She turned the tap on full and splashed her face.

Meanwhile I tried to scoop out the fish so I could clean its bowl. "Guinevere, stop wiggling," I ordered.

"Denise, I need help! Can you take the bowl and pour out the water?"

"But the fish is still swimming in it."

"Don't worry," I said. "I'll catch her and hold her—while you refill the bowl."

Denise frowned. "Chlorinated water will kill the fish."

"Never mind," I snapped. "I have drops to put in so it won't. Now just pour, will you? But *slowly*."

Denise slicked her wet hair back from her face with both hands, then took the bowl.

"Slower," I said. "You're pouring too fast."

"The bowl is wet . . . *difficult* to hold . . ."

"Denise! It's slipping—"

". . . *can't hold it* . . . WATCH OUT!"

The bowl shot past my open hands. It smashed onto the bottom of the sink with a crash.

"Guinevere!" I screamed. The water gurgled down the drain as I gingerly lifted bits of broken glass. But it was too late!

"Oh my gosh," Denise gasped. "The fish . . ." She pointed at the drain.

I felt like crying. "What will I tell Puddy?"

"A pity that that eccentric with the parrot lives so far away," said Denise. "You could always say the macaw swooped down, grabbed the fish, and swallowed it."

I glared at her. "Very funny." I peered into the sink. "Talk about money going down the drain. Poor Guinevere. Hope she makes it to the ocean."

"Possibly Floyd will catch her when he goes down to Baja tomorrow," Denise said.

I didn't bother to answer. After we carefully picked up

the pieces of broken glass and dumped them in the trash, I stormed out.

Denise hurried after me. "Where are you going now?"

"To the pet shop. To buy another fish. *And* a fishbowl. *And* a leather leash for Hilda." I didn't even want to think what this would do to my savings. "I just hope Mr. Willy-Bones lets me charge them all."

"M.D.K., I am *dreadfully* sorry." Denise ran along beside me, trying to keep up. "It was really stupid not to wipe my hands before I reached for that bowl."

I didn't answer. Maybe taking Denise on as a partner was a *big* mistake.

3

The Sheriff Arrives

"SORRY." MR. WILLY-BONES SHOOK HIS HEAD. "I have no more goldfish." His accent turned "have" into "haf."

"This morning you had *lots*," I said. "Where'd they all go?"

"A teacher bought everyone . . . for prizes at a school carnival." The shopkeeper poured himself a cup of coffee from a blue enamel pot, then returned the pot to the hot plate behind the counter and gave me a big smile. "I get more next week."

I looked at Denise. "The Kenilworths get back tomorrow. If I don't find a fish for Puddy, his mom will blab what happened to the whole town . . . and *ruin* my reputation."

Her eyes lit up. "Where is the carnival? Perhaps we could go and win back one of the fish. I am *terrific* at ring toss—"

"That's dumb, Denise! Besides, what if we didn't win?"

She moved to the fish tank. "You could always substitute a tropical fish."

"But Guinevere's a *goldfish*!"

"Merely explain to Puddy how you gave her such excellent care that she changed. He will never suspect."

18

"For a three-year-old, Puddy's pretty smart," I told her. "He'll know. So will his mom." Still, what choice did I have?

"Okay," I told Mr. Willy-Bones. "I'd like your cheapest tropical fish—and one bowl."

With a small net he scooped out a shimmering red fish with brilliant purple markings.

Denise nodded. "Definitely more attractive then Guinevere."

"Also smaller," I said. "Puddy'll know it's not his."

"Simply tell him she molted—and shrank," Denise said. Then she went to the bulletin board.

When Mr. Willy-Bones gave me the bill along with the fish in its bowl of water, I gasped, "Twelve dollars? For one fish?"

"The others cost even more," he said.

I was hoping Denise might offer to pay. She didn't.

"Can I charge it—till tomorrow?" I asked Mr. Willy-Bones. "Now that I have a partner, I expect to get lots of new clients this afternoon. And I'm asking them to pay in advance."

"So you have the money tomorrow?" The old Swede's eyes narrowed over the tops of his wire spectacles. "For sure?"

I nodded.

"Yah, well." His blue eyes sparkled. "All right."

"Thanks!" Clutching the fishbowl, I hurried to the back of the shop. "Denise—want to see Ringo before we go?"

I pressed my face against the bars of his cage. The green parakeet fluttered to me. His red hooked beak almost touched my nose. "Hi, Ringo," I said.

"Hi!" he piped. "Hi!"

"Sorry. No time for a lesson today," I told him. "But are you practicing how to say 'good-bye'?"

"Good! Hi!" he said.

"No. Not 'hi.' 'Bye'!''

"Not! Hi! Bye!" Ringo repeated, blinking his black eyes.

"Forget it," I said. "See you tomorrow."

As I turned from the cage, Mr. Willy-Bones came toward me.

"Margaret," he said. "I have bad news."

It was hard to keep my lips from quivering. "About Ringo?"

"Yah. A man from the bird zoo at Thousand Oaks wants him. I must let him know by Saturday."

I stared at Mr. Willy-Bones. "That's only . . . five days. I'll never have the money by then."

"You know our arrangement." His voice was gentle. "Such a rare bird I cannot keep forever. Every day he loses me money. He takes up space . . . food . . . my time. . . . " He paused. "Your mama and papa maybe could help?"

"They're not even here. Dad's in Oklahoma. And who knows where Mom is by now? The Oregon border maybe."

With pudgy fingers the shopowner stroked his white goatee. "Maybe that nice Texas lady who's visiting you?"

"Shirlee Alabama . . . the sitter?" I snorted. "She's too tightfisted to lend me five cents."

Denise edged past us to look at Ringo. "You are right, M.D.K. He is *definitely* handsomer than Floyd's cockatoos."

The shopowner's eyebrows shot up. "You have cockatoos?"

"Not me. My stepdad," Denise said. "But he sold them."

"Ah. I would like to meet your stepfather some day."

They discussed Floyd and his cockatoos; I blinked back

my tears. Five days! How could I ever earn enough to pay for Ringo in that short time?

"Yah," Mr. Willy-Bones was telling Denise. "Cockatoos are beautiful birds. Worth a lot of money."

She shrugged. "Floyd never said anything about that."

Watching her, I tried to imagine how it would feel to be so rich, you didn't care what things cost. Denise was lucky. Suddenly she grabbed my arm, nearly knocking the fishbowl to the floor.

"Speaking of money, M.D.K.—come and see this!"

She pushed me toward the bulletin board and pointed to the notice. " 'Five-hundred-dollar reward!' " she said. " 'For information leading to the arrest of the smugglers.' What do you think?"

BIRD
SMUGGLERS
$500
REWARD!

"I know. They're the ones I told you about. But we'd never find them." I frowned. "Denise, we don't stand a chance."

"We *do*," she insisted. "Look. It says, 'Operating in Southern California, possibly Malibu.' Practically in our very *midst*!"

Mr. Willy-Bones hurried over. "No, girls. That is not for you. To pursue those smugglers is a dangerous business."

"But *somebody* has to catch them," Denise said.

"Not you two." Mr. Willy-Bones shook his head. "You children should not get mixed up with those bad guys—"

"But they are so mean to those parrots," interrupted Denise. "They drug them to keep them quiet. They tape their beaks shut—"

"Yah, yah." Mr. Willy-Bones nodded and gave Denise a funny look. "How do you know so much about this?"

"Floyd subscribed to *stacks* of wildlife magazines when he was raising cockatoos," she said. "They contained dozens of articles about bird smuggling."

"I could use the reward," I said, still studying the notice. "But where would we start looking?"

"I won't have it!" Mr. Willy-Bones stomped his foot. "You must *not*—" A ringing telephone stopped his lecture. Still shaking his head, he went to answer.

"It is imperative, first of all," Denise said, "that we devise a strategy to trap these criminal types."

"Like what?" I asked. "Setting up a roadblock? How can the two of us do that, Denise? It's crazy."

As Mr. Willy-Bones talked on the phone, he was still watching us and shaking his head.

"Not all smuggling is done with cars," Denise said. "We could stake out Santa Monica Airport, just south of here. Isn't that where your mother keeps her plane?"

"Sure—except Mom's not here. Besides, if these guys are breaking the law, they're not going to land at a public airport." Denise might be a brain, but she didn't know everything. "They'll land out in the desert or in an empty field someplace."

"True," she agreed. "Perhaps a wiser strategy is to check out various pet shops—and nab them as they try to sell the birds."

"It'd take forever," I said. "Let's stick with pet-sitting. Now let's get this fish up the hill before it dies on us."

This time Denise kept up with me climbing Puddy's hill. The reason was that I had to go slow to keep from spilling the water out of the fishbowl. Halfway up the hill she smiled and reached out for the bowl. "Want me to carry that for a while?"

"Thanks, but no thanks." I held tight to it. Another round of buying fish and glass bowls and I'd be broke.

By about four thirty we had delivered Puddy's fish and were heading back down the hill. Again Denise tried to persuade me to hunt the smugglers.

"It would be such a challenge," she said. "And with your *vast* experience outwitting those smugglers in Texas—"

"I also got kidnapped, don't forget," I reminded her.

"It would be much more exciting than changing kitty litter."

"Tending Conrad the Clawless Cat isn't my job now, anyway," I said. "It's yours."

Then Denise said something really strange.

"It *is* peculiar," she said, "how reluctant the shop-owner was to discuss the smuggling operation. *And* the way he discouraged us from becoming involved."

"Mr. Willy-Bones just doesn't want us to get hurt," I said.

"Perhaps."

"Denise, you're not accusing *him* of smuggling?"

"Not exactly. But we should remain alert to all possi-bilities. The smuggler could be *anybody*—one of your cus-tomers, even." She ran a hand through her thick dark hair. "Did any of them go to Australia? Or South America? Those countries are the source of most smuggled exotic birds."

I began to laugh. "Mrs. Eastley's in Iowa, visiting her sister," I said. "Kim's at camp. The Kenilworths's—"

Denise acted hurt. "I merely suggested we keep our eyes and ears open."

"Tell you what," I said. "If you promise to help me find more pet clients—I promise to *think* about hunting the smugglers. But *after* I get Ringo paid for."

Denise cocked her head like she was deciding. Then she smiled. "Agreed," she said.

So we stopped at every house we passed with a dog or cat in the yard. I gave out business cards with my new motto to the owners. People were friendly. But no one needed our services.

We had no better luck at the park. All we found were kids playing soccer. We stopped to sit on the library steps. But here all we saw were kids with books.

"A smuggler hunt would produce more results," said Denise.

"Produce! I almost forgot." I jumped up. "Mr. Parducci, the produce man at the market, is saving carrot tops for me, for the rabbit. I have to pick them up." I started toward downtown. "What time is it?"

Denise glanced at her orange Swatch watch. "Almost six."

"Forget the market." I spun around and headed the other direction. "I'm going home. I promised to be back at six."

As I hurried toward my house, Denise ran after me. "But there are *hours* of daylight remaining. . . ."

"You don't know Shirlee Alabama. That woman's a . . ." I searched for a Denise-type word. "A menace! If I'm home late, she'll have the police out searching."

"You must be kidding. Nobody would call the police."

"*She* would. Her name may be Shirlee, but she's a Nervous Nellie."

"Wait, M.D.K.! Tomorrow . . . when I walk Hilda . . . what about her leash?"

Drat! I had forgotten all about buying a new leash when I was at the pet shop. Denise would need one. "Use rope."

"But I have . . . no rope." Denise tried to keep up as I hurried ahead. "And what about her food?"

I stopped to wait. "Maybe you'd better come home with

me," I said. "We have clothesline rope. And I can give you puppy biscuits and write out the instructions—"

"Is it *that* complicated?" she said. "Maybe I should not—"

"Oh, no," I said quickly. I didn't want her to back out now. "It's just to—to make sure you know what to do. Why not stay for dinner? I can explain then. That is, if you don't mind chili. That's about all Shirlee ever cooks."

Denise grinned as she started walking again. "I dislike it only with peanut butter."

"You can call your mom from my house," I said.

"Mother seldom worries . . . about my whereabouts." Denise stopped to catch her breath. "Anyway . . . she will be at the club . . . until late . . . and Floyd will be . . . at the beach house."

As I waited, I wondered what it would be like to have parents who didn't care what you did. Might be fun. And I could certainly use a sitter who didn't worry so much "about my whereabouts."

Then I heard the clock in the schoolhouse tower, far below. It chimed six. I broke into a run. "Hurry!"

"I can scarcely *walk*," she gasped, "let alone *run*."

So we covered the last three blocks at a slow crawl. When we got to my block, I saw a black-and-white police car back out of our driveway. No, not the police. It was the county sheriff!

"Your sitter did it," said Denise, fixing her eyes on the black-and-white. "She really *did* call the police."

Then she gripped my shoulders. "You are in for it now, M.D.K.!"

4

A Secret and a Clue

IN THE DOORWAY SHIRLEE ALABAMA CRISSCROSSED her arms. I stared. Who was she signaling? I glanced around. Already the black-and-white car was halfway to the corner. If her signal was for the sheriff—too bad. But no, the skinny arms still flapped.

"She must be waving at *me*," I told Denise. "And she's *smiling*!"

"Hurry—we're just fixin' to sit down," Shirlee called. "There's company for supper."

Then I saw Wil Bradley behind her. I grabbed Denise's arm and started to run. "Come on—it's Wil, my friend from Texas!" When we rushed in, Wil gave me that slow, friendly grin of his.

"Howdy, M.D.K.," he drawled.

"Wil! What are you doing in California?"

He hadn't changed. Still a skinny thirteen-year-old with those same knobby knees. And he was wearing California-style surfer shorts! He ducked his head. "My dad had this meeting—"

"Law officers' convention," bellowed Sheriff Bradley from the E-Z lounger. "In Anaheim," he added importantly.

Wil nodded. "I'd never seen the Pacific Ocean—so Dad brought me along."

The sheriff eased himself out of the chair and stood, thumbs hooked in his belt. "All it cost was young Wil's ticket . . . since we're staying with my cousin Pete."

Wil nodded. "Pete's in law enforcement too."

The sheriff broke in. "Well, tarnation, Pete lives in Santa Monica—so close I could almost *smell* Miz Alabama's chili. So I decided to call up and wangle a supper invite."

Shirlee beamed. "I told 'em to come right on over."

That explained the black-and-white squad car.

"I'll tell you one thing, young lady." Sheriff Bradley winked at me. "Riverbank, Texas, hasn't been the same since Shirlee Alabama left. We miss that good Tex-Mex of hers."

"Wilson Bradley, the *way* you *talk*." Shirlee patted her flaming-red topknot, then nudged him and Wil toward the dining table. It was set with Mom's linen tablecloth and china, plus her best silverware, which we bring out only for holidays and birthdays. If Mom knew, she would have kittens!

"You-all set yourselves down," Shirlee said. "And do your talkin' while you eat." Clamping her thin lips into a smile, she turned to me. "Sweetie, if your friend's stayin', find her a chair—" Suddenly the sitter's sharp nose quivered. "*My lordy*, the biscuits." With a shriek she flew to the kitchen.

Wil grinned at me from across the table. "What're you doing these days, M.D.K.? Solving more mysteries?"

Denise looked at me and began bobbing her chin up and down.

I ignored her. "Mostly earning money to buy a parakeet."

Wil smiled. "No more prairie dogs?" Then his face clouded. "Sorry to hear about ol' Gertrude passing on."

"Geraldine the Third *was* old for a hamster," I said. "But now she's up in hamster heaven, with Geraldines One and Two. For a change I'm getting a bird. One that talks!"

"An Indian ringneck parakeet," added Denise. I remembered that I hadn't introduced her to everyone, so I did.

"Do you live around here, honey?" Shirlee asked, breezing in. Without waiting for Denise's reply, she plopped a basket of steaming biscuits on the table, saying, "Help yourself. Plenty more where these came from." Then she shoved the Crockpot in front of the sheriff. "There's more chili, too, so dig in."

For the rest of the meal Shirlee, the sheriff, and sometimes Wil gabbed about Texas with accents as thick as the sorghum they slathered on their biscuits. My only chance to talk with Wil was when Shirlee left to load up the biscuit basket and refill the Crockpot. Denise was too busy gulping water between bites of the fiery chili to talk at all.

"Don't worry," I whispered to her. "When Mom and I went to Riverbank and I tasted Shirlee's Tex-Mex for the first time, it took three quarts of iced tea to get through the meal!"

Dessert was pecan pie. After finishing off a second slice, Sheriff Bradley pushed away from the table, burped, and patted his belly. "You're one mighty fine cook, Miz Alabama."

Then he winked at me. "How soon you gonna let this lady come back to Riverbank to open up her café again?"

"In a couple of weeks," I said. "When my folks get home."

Shirlee dabbed her lips with her linen napkin. "I may not go back to Texas," she said. "I may stay here."

The sheriff stared at her, the only time I'd seen him speechless.

Wil wasn't shy about speaking up. "If I lived this close to the ocean," he said, "I'd stay too—take up surfing!"

I looked at Denise and giggled. I could just see Shirlee Alabama on a surfboard.

Then Shirlee pursed her lips like she had a great secret. "Oh, it's not the ocean." But that was all she would say.

I jumped up from the table. "I want to show my bird cage to Denise and Wil."

When Wil stood, the sheriff rested a beefy hand on his shoulder. "Look fast, son. Pete's pickin' us up at nine."

"That reminds me," I told Denise. "Don't you want to call your folks? The phone's in the kitchen."

Denise scooted her chair back. "What time should I tell them to pick me up?"

"Nine's fine," I told her. After she left, I said to Wil, "Did you ever watch *Uncle Floyd's Kiddie Brigade* on TV?"

"Sometimes."

"Floyd's her stepdad."

"No kidding?" Wil scrunched his nose. "It's kind of a dumb show, though."

Shirlee stopped scraping plates to listen. "I've seen that program. It was kinda clever, I thought." She gave a twittery laugh. "That Floyd is *so* funny. And to think that sweet little girl's his daughter!"

When Denise came back, we started for my room. But Shirlee blocked the way. Now she made up for not paying attention to Denise earlier. "Why, honey," she cooed, "I had no *idea* that darling Uncle Floyd on the TV was your daddy—"

"Stepdad," Denise said.

Shirlee pursed her thin lips. "It's my very favorite show."

Denise shrugged. "They are all reruns. It has been *years* since Floyd did a new show."

"Don't matter. He's still funny." Shirlee's eyes were about to pop out of her head. "Will your daddy be pickin' you up?"

"My mother, probably. Floyd had to prepare for his fishing trip tomorrow."

Sheriff Bradley's voice boomed from the living room. "You say your stepdaddy's goin' fishin' tomorrow? So are me and Pete. We're goin' over to Catalina."

"Floyd is going to Baja, California," Denise said. "It is a part of Mexico."

"What's he usually catch?" the sheriff asked.

"Usually nothing," she said.

Denise trailed Wil and me down the hall. "M.D.K., how could you call your sitter a 'menace'?" she asked. "I think she is *quaint*. And that pecan pie was *fabulous*!"

"First time she's made anything besides baked apples for dessert," I said. "She's just on her good behavior because of her Texas friends."

I kicked aside some old jeans and one slipper in the doorway to my room and led Wil and Denise in.

Wil frowned. "Wonder why ol' Shirlee decided not to go back home?"

Denise giggled. "She may have acquired a California boyfriend."

"Her?" I said. "She must be past seventy."

"Perhaps the boyfriend is too."

"If she stays, it won't be in *my* house," I said. "The minute Mom and Dad get back, she goes."

As Wil started to sink into my beanbag chair, I pulled at his arm. "First take a look at Ringo's cage." Then I explained, "That's my parakeet's name."

Wil ambled to the ornate metal cage that covered half

of my dresser top. "It's fancy all right. Old Jingo'll love it. Where'd you get it?"

"At Goodwill. After I give it a good scrubbing, it'll look even better."

Denise wrinkled her nose. "A new paint job will definitely improve it."

"Oh, *no*!" I said. "You *never* paint bird cages. The paint might be poisonous. If your bird pecked at it, he could die."

Denise stuck her nose in the air. She seemed hurt that I knew something she didn't. "Anyway," she said, "I don't believe in caging birds. *I* think wild creatures should remain in the forest, where they belong."

"Is your parakeet wild, M.D.K.?" Wil asked.

"Maybe his ancestors in India were—but Ringo's tame." I looked at Denise. "And he doesn't mind being in a cage at the pet shop."

"How can you be *sure*?" Denise demanded.

It was hard to answer her—because I *wasn't* sure. "At least nobody smuggled him into this country in some woman's nylon stocking," I said. "Like they do with baby parrots."

"Nevertheless, I suspect his captors—"

"Ringo didn't *have* a captor," I told her. "Mr. Willy-Bones told me that practically all Indian ringneck parakeets are raised in this country now—including Ringo."

Denise sniffed and went to the windowsill where I keep my shell collection.

"So what's ol' Ringtail look like?" Wil asked me.

"Not 'Ringtail.' *Ringo!*" I pretended to be angry, but I knew Wil was only teasing. "And he's not mine till he's paid for. Want to see the picture I drew?" I reached into the cage for my sketch of Ringo. "Don't mind the smudges," I said. "But he looks like this. Only prettier. The feathers make a ring around his neck."

Wil whistled through his teeth as he studied what I'd drawn. "You're still a good artist, M.D.K.!" He smiled. "Remember that picture of old Gladys you sent me? I've still got it!"

"Who is Gladys?" Denise asked, coming over to look.

"He means Geraldine the Third. He has this problem with names."

I made a face at Wil. He just stood there, grinning.

Denise gave me a kind of half smile like she wanted to be friends again. She nodded toward the sketch. "That *is* good, M.D.K. Instead of sitting pets, you should do pet portraits. You would have Ringo paid for in no time."

"What's this Marvelous Mingo cost?" Wil asked.

"Seventy-five dollars," I said.

He whistled. "This must be one *rare* bird."

"Come back tomorrow and you can meet him," I said. "Only promise you won't teach him a Texas drawl."

Wil shook his head. "Tomorrow my cousins are showing me around L.A." Then he grinned. "Want to come along?"

"Can't. We have pets to care for." I started to list them.

"But no more fish, remember?" Denise said as she went back to examining my shells. "The Kenilworths return tomorrow."

I nodded. Both Denise and I began talking at once as we told Wil about our troubles with Puddy's goldfish. Then I told Wil how the Parrot Man's pet macaw had attacked Hilda.

He laughed. "Sounds like this pet-sitting is a mighty dangerous business."

"At least now I have a partner," I said. "That will help."

Denise shuddered. "Now *I* must cope with the Parrot Man."

I looked from Denise to Wil. Suddenly I got this great

idea. If one partner was good, two might be even better. "Want to come with us, Wil? With you along, we'd finish even sooner. And you could help us find new customers."

He rubbed his chin. "I was hopin' to see the sights of the big city tomorrow. My cousins made all these plans."

"Be realistic, M.D.K." Denise waved a sand dollar. "Even with three of us, we *still* might not find any new clients. If it is like today, we may not find any."

I hated to admit it, but she was right. I put Ringo's sketch back in the cage. Was a picture of him all I'd ever have?

Denise cocked her head. "What *I* think your friend should do is assist us in finding the parrot smugglers. After all, you two did manage to track down those criminal types in Texas—"

"Did you say parrot smugglers?" Wil's brown eyes lit up.

Denise nodded. "And there is a five-hundred-dollar reward for finding them."

"All *right*!" Wil's whole face was one big, toothy grin. "After we find 'em, M.D.K., you take part of the reward and buy your talking Bingo. On what's left we'll all go to Disneyland!"

"What do you mean, '*after* we find them'? Who says we will?"

"I'll bet we can do it!" he said.

"Of course we can." Denise looked over at me. "With three of us working on the problem, we are bound to succeed."

I stared into the empty cage. I remembered what Mr. Willy-Bones had told me: only five days to come up with the money for Ringo. I sighed. It looked like the reward was my only chance.

"All right," I said.

"*Stupendous!*" Denise shouted, waving her arms. Then

her elbow knocked against the box of seashells. Down it fell.

"Oh, M.D.K. I'm *dreadfully* sorry."

I fell to my knees to examine the damage. "At least my favorite star shell survived," I said. I felt bad about the broken sand dollars. But it was my own fault. I should never have let Denise get near those shells. I should have aimed her toward my stuffed-animal collection. It would have been safer.

Wil stood by the bird cage. He looked like his dad as he hooked his thumbs over the waistband of his surfer shorts. "If y'all want to get that reward," he drawled, "we'd better get started."

Denise sat sedately on the edge of my bed, hands in her lap. I perched beside her. "It's okay about the shells," I whispered. "I had too many anyway."

"So what clues do you have so far?" Wil asked.

I shook my head. "None."

"Yes, we do." Denise turned to look at me. "For one thing, we know they are operating in this area. And also the pet-shop owner is *definitely* a suspect."

I snorted. "Not Mr. Willy-Bones."

"He did attempt to prevent us from getting involved."

I jumped up. "Denise! He was only afraid we'd get hurt."

"He may have *said* that. But how do we—"

"Hold on!" interrupted Wil. "When my dad's on a case, I do believe he puts *everybody* on his suspect list— to start with, anyway. And every clue. We should too." Wil looked at me. "Got that famous notebook of yours, Detective Kincaid?"

I went to my desk to grab a colored pencil and my sketchbook. "So what do I write?"

"Under suspects: Mr. Wilhelm Bjornson," said Denise.

I glared at her.

"Won't hurt to put it down just for now," said Wil.

So I wrote "Willy-Bones"—but lightly, so it would be easy to erase. I knew *he* wasn't involved with those bad guys.

"Now," said Wil. "What about this dude with the nasty-tempered parrot?"

"He *could* be a suspect," I said, and I wrote "Parrot Man" in my notebook.

Wil walked back and forth. It was fun being a detective with him again. And Denise was going to make a terrific partner too. But even with three of us on the case, would we ever solve it?

Wil still paced, thumbs hooked on his waistband. "Any idea how the smugglers are getting here?" he asked.

"If they come from Mexico," Denise said, "it could be by car or bus or truck."

I wrote as she talked.

"Or airplane," I said, writing that down too. "Or boat."

Then I stopped scribbling. I slapped my sketchbook closed. "This is impossible. How can we cover every airport and boat landing and road and bus station around here?"

"Perhaps a better scheme is to capture the criminals when they unload their contraband."

"Talk normal, Denise!" I said.

"What I *mean*," she said, "is when they sell the baby birds through newspaper ads or to pet dealers."

Wil nodded. "It'd be a cinch to stake out pet shops. Then when the guys deliver the birds, we nab them."

"Not that easy," I said. "Lots of places sell pets. Besides Mr. Willy-Bones, there's a store in Malibu. And dozens in Santa Monica. We can't cover them all. I *do* still have my own pet clients to feed, you know."

Suddenly I remembered the greens for the rabbit. I turned to Denise. "I *knew* we should have picked up those carrot tops this afternoon. By tomorrow Mr. Parducci will have thrown them out."

"We could go to the market now," Denise said. "My mother will not come until nine."

"So let's go!" I grabbed my pack. "C'mon, Wil."

We dashed for the front door. But Shirlee stood before it, blocking our way.

"It's after eight," she told me. "Can't let you go out so late. Your mama wouldn't approve."

"Just to the market," I protested. "It's not even dark yet. And with three of us we'll be safe."

From the E-Z lounger the sheriff said, "Miz Alabama, you worry too much. Let 'em go. But remember, son," he warned Wil, "you be back here by nine."

Shirlee reluctantly moved away from the door. We ran out and raced down the hill. When we burst into the storage room at the back of the market, Mr. Parducci was talking on the phone. He pointed toward a couple of grocery bags overflowing with greens that rested against a stack of wooden crates.

I nodded thanks. Wil helped me stuff the bags into my pack while Denise wandered among the boxes of fruits and vegetables. When we were on the street again, she grabbed my arm.

"Did you notice what was on those wooden tomato crates?"

"I didn't see anything," I said.

"Me neither," said Wil.

Denise looked all around. "I have reason to believe," she whispered, "that we have located our smuggler."

5

A Mysterious Phone Call

CLIMBING UP THE HILL TOOK THREE TIMES AS LONG as it had racing down it. Wil, with his long strides, had no trouble, but Denise kept straggling behind. Every two blocks we stopped to wait. Each time she caught up, she again tried to convince Wil and me that old Mr. Parducci was the smuggler.

"But those crates from Mexico . . . It's *obvious*," she insisted. "What better way to smuggle baby parrots?"

"Or ship tomatoes." I glared at Denise, wishing she'd skip the detective nonsense and hurry up the hill.

"That Puccini guy looked harmless to me," said Wil.

"*Furtive*," Denise said. "That is how he appeared to me. Did you *notice* how he covered the receiver when we came in? Undoubtedly phoning his cohorts."

"But you have no proof," I said. For a smart kid Denise sometimes was really dense. Not until we reached home could Wil and I persuade her that Mr. Parducci wasn't a parrot pirate.

The grandfather's clock that my dad built struck nine as we burst through the front doorway. Shirlee stood waiting.

"I was about to send for the po-lice," she said, "I was so worried." Behind her the sheriff chuckled.

A car horn sounded, and Denise bounded back out, saying, "That will be for me."

I followed her to the white Mercedes that had pulled into the drive. Shirlee trotted after me, but returned to the porch when she discovered it was Denise's mother and not Floyd at the wheel.

"Hurry up, Denny," Mrs. Barker called.

As Denise jumped into the front seat, I said, "The dog food's in a metal can by Mrs. Eastley's back door." Then I shrieked, "Wait! You forgot Hilda's leash."

I raced to Dad's workshop for a hank of clothesline rope. "This'll have to do!" I told Denise, thrusting the rope at her through the open car window. "See you in the morning."

When I hurried back to the house, Wil and his dad were on the front porch. "But, Dad," Wil was saying. "I'd rather help M.D.K. feed her pets tomorrow."

"Suit yourself, son," the sheriff replied. "It's your vacation. But how are you gettin' up here from Santa Monica?"

I broke in. "There's a bus every half hour." I smiled at Wil, hoping he had not told his dad too much about our plans. The sheriff might not mind, but Shirlee would. If she knew I was on the trail of smugglers, she'd have a conniption fit.

A black-and-white squad car pulled to the curb. As Wil slid into the squad car with his dad, I told him, "Take bus number fifty-six. . . . It goes along Sunset Boulevard. Get off at Ocean Street. I'll meet you there at ten."

After Shirlee and I went back into the house, she settled in front of the television. But I went into my room and closed my door. So much had happened today, good and bad, that I needed to sort it out. The bad news was the man from the bird zoo wanting to buy Ringo on Saturday.

Today was Tuesday. That didn't give me much time to earn enough to buy the parakeet myself.

I took off my mud-spattered T-shirt and shorts and slipped into my nightie. Then I brought Sinclair, my dinosaur bank, from his hiding place on my closet shelf. Settling in my beanbag chair, I began to add up my savings. I counted the coins and the bills three times, but the answer always came out the same: $32.28. And out of that had to come twelve dollars to pay Mr. Willy-Bones for the fish and the bowl, and maybe another five for Hilda's leash.

I'd be lucky to end up with fifteen dollars. Denise was right. My only hope was to go for the reward.

Wil's arrival was definitely good news. With his help maybe we *could* find the smugglers.

But Denise was another story. It was unfair to call her bad news, but losing Puddy's fish down the drain wasn't what you'd call helpful. Neither was spilling my shell collection. Still, she did have some good ideas. And anyway, sand dollars are like four-leaf clovers. The fun part is finding them.

I yawned and pushed myself out of the beanbag chair. After putting Sinclair away, I switched off my light and climbed into bed. I lay in the dark, outlining plans to catch smugglers, but the more I planned, the dumber the idea seemed. How could we find the smugglers in three days? We didn't even know where to start looking. And if the best suspect we could come up with was Mr. Parducci, we ought to give up. I should forget about Ringo and settle for another hamster.

I squeezed my eyes shut, and to make myself fall asleep counted hamsters jumping over a Lincoln Log fence. It didn't work. Finally I got up. A piece of Shirlee's pecan pie and a glass of milk might make me sleepy.

As I padded along the hall, I heard the television blaring

in the dark living room. Had Shirlee forgotten to switch it
off when she'd gone to bed?

Under the kitchen door a light shone. When I put my
hand on the door to push it open, I heard Shirlee's voice.
She was talking on the phone—but not with her usual loud
cackle. Her voice was soft. Was she worried I might hear?

Instead of barging in, I hesitated. Her quiet tone made
me curious.

". . . I'll be ready . . . Friday at twelve . . . and don't
you forget the extry containers!''

Containers? For what?

Abruptly Shirlee said, "All righty, Jerome. Talk to you
tomorrow.'' I spun around and raced to my room before
she caught me eavesdropping.

But who was Jerome? And what was happening Friday
at twelve?

6

A Startling Discovery

THE NEXT MORNING I WAS WAITING AT THE CORNER of Sunset and Ocean as the clock in the school tower bonged for the tenth time. The bus from Santa Monica eased to the curb. The door hissed open. First I saw Wil's knobby knees beneath oversized cutoffs, then the rest of his skinny frame as he leaped onto the sidewalk.

That big grin spread across his freckled face. "Find the smugglers yet, M.D.K.?"

"Hardly. I've been feeding pets since seven. And I'm still not done."

"Guess it helped for your friend to walk that little dachsie."

I nodded. "And now she takes care of Conrad the cat, too. She 'a-dooooores' cats."

Wil scratched his head. "*And* high-powered words. Doesn't she know any with one syllable?"

"A few."

Wil smiled. "So when do I get to see ol' Gringo?"

"When we get to the pet shop. And his name's Ringo."

As we walked, Wil held out the paper bag he carried. "Want a doughnut?"

"Thanks." I reached into the bag. "All I had for breakfast was a gulp of milk and an orange."

"Doesn't ol' Shirlee insist you eat your morning oatmeal?"

"Shirlee wasn't even there when I got up," I said.

"Where'd she go?"

"No idea. It's too early for the market or the Senior Center. They're the only places she ever goes."

Wil snickered. "Maybe she really does have a secret admirer."

"She's got a secret *something*," I said, and I told Wil about the mysterious phone call. "She talked about 'containers.' And what kind of a meeting do you think it would be on Friday with this Jerome, whoever *he* is?"

Wil shrugged. "No idea." He offered me the last doughnut, but I shook my head.

"That phone call can't mean much," he went on. "Shirlee's a good ol' bat."

"It might have to do with her staying here," I said. "Instead of going back to Texas."

"Could be." Wil stuffed the doughnut into his mouth and crumpled the bag.

"In the next block there's a trash can," I said. "In front of Delia's Beauty Parlor."

The pet shop was a half block beyond Delia's. As we approached, Denise ran toward us, waving her arms.

"Catastrophe!" she screamed. *"Catastrophe!"*

"What's wrong?" I yelled as we raced to meet her.

"It is too dreadful," she gasped. "Hilda is missing!"

"Wasn't she there this morning?" I asked.

Denise nodded, tears streaming down her cheeks. "It happened after I fed her. . . . I tied the rope to her collar . . . we started walking . . ."

"So how'd she get away?"

"I forgot to replace the lid on the food can," said Denise. "After tying Hilda to a bush, I went back to cover it. . . . When I returned . . . she had disappeared! Oh, M.D.K., I am *devastated*. How can you ever forgive—''

''Forget the flowery apologies,'' I snapped. ''We've got to find that dog.''

We raced west along Ocean Street to Edgecliff Road, where Mrs. Eastley lived. When we reached her yard, I turned to Denise.

''Where, exactly, did you last see Hilda?''

Denise pointed. ''Next to that oleander bush.''

''She must have gone into the Parrot Man's yard,'' I said.

''But I called through the hedge,'' said Denise. ''There was no answer. So I investigated in the tall weeds around Mrs. Eastley's house. I searched for an *hour*.''

Wil strode toward the open field in back of the house. ''How far away is the beach?''

''Just past the cliff edge—and two hundred feet straight down,'' I said.

''Is there a path to the beach?'' asked Wil.

I nodded. ''A *steep* one.''

''How absolutely *dreadful*!'' Denise wailed. ''If she ran down to the Coast Highway, with all that traffic she would *never* survive.''

I glared at her. That's all I needed to make my day: one dead dog.

''We oughta check out that neighbor with the parrot,'' Wil said.

''But I called through the hedge,'' protested Denise.

''I agree with Wil,'' I said. ''If the parrot cornered poor Hilda again, she might be too scared to bark.''

Wil started back toward the street. ''So let's go rescue her.''

I admired Wil. He had courage. I knew that from when we tangled with those Texas smugglers. And now he sounded braver than I felt. Still, if Hilda was in that yard,

I had to save her. I had no choice. Following Wil to the Parrot Man's front gate, I kept repeating, "I'm not scared, I'm not scared."

Wil pushed open the gate, and the three of us stepped inside. As on the day before, all was quiet. I scanned the garden and small shed at the back. Was the Parrot Man hiding, waiting to spring on us? I eyed his cottage. It looked empty, but could we be sure?

"There she *is*!" screamed Denise.

Hilda crept out from under a pile of boards. Wil pounced on the trembling dog. He held her while I slipped the rope under her collar and tied it with a strong knot. Then I nuzzled the little sausage dog.

"Hilda! Why do you keep coming over here?" I stood and gave the rope a tug.

"Come on," I called to Denise. "Let's take Hilda home."

"Wait." Denise was rummaging through a pile of wood scraps. "There might be valuable evidence. After all, the Parrot Man is on our suspect list."

"Even more reason to not get caught," I said. "That old man could be inside his house, you know."

Suddenly Wil whistled. "Cowboys' bumpers! Get a load of the snakeskin tacked on that old shack—"

He charged toward the shed by the Parrot Man's back fence. Denise threw down the wood scraps and joined him.

"Incredible," she said. "A *diamondback rattler*."

"Come back!" I shouted, but by now Wil was bounding up the ladder to the roof of the shed. He gave a loud whoop.

"Hey, M.D.K.!" he called. "Here's a telescope."

"Forget it!" I yelled. "Let's go before the Parrot Man catches us."

Ignoring my warning, Wil bent to peer through the eyepiece. "I can see the beach." He swiveled the telescope. "And there's the lifeguard tower."

Denise scrambled up the ladder. Wil back away to let her look. *"Spectacular!"* she squealed. "You can see our beach house in Malibu."

"You've got a beach house up there? Let me have a look." Wil tried to elbow her aside.

"Wait. I want to see if Floyd's boat is still anchored offshore," she said. "No, it appears he has already gone." She stepped back to give Wil a turn.

"You guys, we're *trespassing!*" I shoved my hands into my jeans pockets and glared at them. "If that man catches us, my whole business is ruined. Nobody'll hire me."

But Wil and Denise weren't even listening. They laughed and chattered as they took turns at the telescope, as if they didn't care about my pet-sitting business at all.

I felt like crying. Instead, I gave Hilda's rope a yank and spun on my heel. "So stay there! But I'm going to finish my rounds."

Then Wil called out. "M.D.K., come back. You're safe."

"What are you talking about?"

"I just saw a wiry little shrimp with a red macaw on his shoulder. Denise says he's the Parrot Man."

"Really?" This I had to see for myself. I rushed back to the shed. Trying to avoid even a glance at the snakeskin, I looped Hilda's rope around the door handle and started up the ladder.

Wil called again. "And M.D.K.—guess who he's talking to? Shirlee Alabama!"

7

The Letter from Brazil

"IS IT REALLY SHIRLEE TALKING WITH THE PARROT Man?"

Wil nodded. "Cowboy's honor."

Hurrying to look through the telescope, I nearly tripped on those red signal flags I'd seen the Parrot Man using. But there was no time to tell Wil about that now. Squinting into the eyepiece, I saw people milling along Malibu Pier—but no one I recognized.

"Where's Shirlee?" I demanded. "I don't see her . . . or him, either."

"They're there," Wil insisted, and whistling through his teeth, took my place. He swiveled the telescope and abruptly stopped whistling.

"Cowboys' bumpers! They're gone!"

I frowned. "You're sure you two didn't make the whole thing up?"

"We did not. *Honestly!*" Denise said. "They must have gone into Sam's Oyster Bar."

"Why would Shirlee do that? She hates oysters," I said. "Besides, she doesn't even know that Parrot Man."

Wil grinned. "I've a hunch he's that secret admirer."

"You and your hunches. Where would she have met him?" I asked, walking back to the ladder. "All she does is look at TV and go to the Senior Center." I started to climb down. "I think we should get away from here while we can."

"But the ol' guy's up in Malibu. I *saw* him," Wil insisted. He wouldn't leave the telescope. He moved it slowly from side to side, trying to locate the Parrot Man and Shirlee.

I was loosening Hilda's rope from the door handle when Denise called down from the roof. "Wait, M.D.K.—I am coming with you."

"Me too," said Wil, giving up the search.

They climbed down quickly. As we hurried across the Parrot Man's yard, I kept glancing at the rundown cottage.

"*Honestly.* He really is in Malibu," said Denise.

"Ol' Shirlee, too," said Wil. "I'm sure of it."

"I believe you—but I still feel funny staying so long in his yard. What if somebody sees us?"

"We'll say we came to get the pooch," said Wil.

I glanced back at the shed. "I wonder why the Parrot Man has that telescope."

"If I lived this close to the ocean, I'd have one too." Wil threw back his shoulders. "Good way to check on smugglers," he said, sounding just like his dad. "If law enforcement's your line of work."

"Or to check on law officers," said Denise slyly, "if smuggling is your line of work."

She picked up the splintered board she'd been examining before. She waved it. "Look. It says 'Mexico.' I will bet *anything* that the Parrot Man—"

"Oh, no!" Wil groaned. "Not another suspect."

I studied the board. "It's from an old crate he probably picked up at the dump for firewood."

"On the contrary," said Denise. "It proves the Parrot Man is dealing in contraband."

I snorted. "First it's poor old Mr. Willy-Bones. Then

Mr. Parducci down at the market. Now it's the Parrot Man. The next thing, Denise, you'll accuse the three of them of being in this together.''

"They could be. However, it is more likely that the Parrot Man operates alone.'' She rapped the wood. "What better evidence do you need? The Parrot Man could be smuggling birds up from Mexico in packing crates. Perhaps that is how he acquired the red macaw.''

"Even if he does bring things across the border, they don't have to be illegal," I said. "Lots of people go to Tijuana to buy stuff. Sometimes my mom travels down to get perfume and those pretty blue hand-blown glasses.''

Denise dropped the board to snatch a gray feather from the ground. She waved it triumphantly. "Proof positive! This *has* to be from a baby parrot.''

"Let's take Hilda home," I said. I didn't have the heart to tell Denise that the feather came from an ordinary, garbage-dump variety sea gull.

Denise pocketed the feather and picked up a stick.

"Trash often contains valuable evidence," she said, poking the stick through the contents of a dented barrel.

She fished out a paper bag. It was covered with coffee grounds and globs of what looked like chili or tomato sauce.

"Yuck!" I held my nose. "Smelly evidence of what the Parrot Man ate for dinner, that's all.''

As Denise dropped the grungy bag into the barrel, I noticed a postcard stuck to it, and also a white envelope pasted with orange-and-green stamps. Thinking of my stamp collection, I grabbed the envelope.

"Let me see that postcard," said Wil. "It might tell us something." But after a glance he flipped the card back in the barrel. "Naw. Just about a get-together in Malibu of some Old-Timer Lifeguard Association.''

I stared at the enveloped in my hand. "This is addressed

to *Jerome Adams*! The person Shirlee talked to last night on the phone was named Jerome.''

Wil was looking over my shoulder. Then he whistled. "Those stamps look foreign. . . . My little brother collects stamps. Can I—''

Denise crowded in. "From Brazil," she said. Her eyes widened. "Nearly *half* the baby parrots smuggled into this country come from the Brazilian jungles. There was this article—'' She turned to Wil. "It described how the trappers pull the baby birds from their nests and ship them to Mexico, where someone else smuggles them into the States.''

Nodding, I wiped the gooey food from the envelope. "This could be important evidence.''

"The Parrot Man's contact!" shouted Denise.

Wil studied the return address. "Rúa Misteriosa, thirteen. A suspicious-sounding address if ever I heard one.''

Denise was jumping up and down. "I was *positive* the Parrot Man was the smuggler!" she shouted. "Absolutely *positive*!''

"Too bad there's no letter inside," I said.

Denise began wildly stirring the trash with a stick. "Perhaps I can locate—''

"No!" I stuffed the envelope into my pack. "We've got to take Hilda home, and then show this to Mr. Willy-Bones—right now!''

8

On the Trail of Evil Eyes

RACING TOWARD THE PET SHOP, WE TRIED TO FIGURE out how the smuggling operation worked.

"The telescope's the key!" Wil's skinny arms flapped every which way. "A boat comes in with smuggled birds. The Parrot Man's at his lookout. He spots it—"

"He signals his contact at Malibu Pier by semaphore," I broke in, remembering the red flags.

"And our evidence is absolutely *incriminating*!" Denise screamed, waving her bedraggled gray feather. "We should inform the authorities right away."

"Mr. Willy-Bones will know who to call," I assured them as we neared the pet shop. And when we burst in, I shouted, "We've *got* to talk to you, Mr. Willy-Bones!"

The shopkeeper turned away from the tall, thin man he was talking to. "Excuse me, Mr. Perry," he said, then added to me, "I'm busy now." His voice had a sharp edge.

I backed away. I didn't like the way this Mr. Perry stared at me, his lips curled in a sneer as he spoke in a high-pitched whine that was almost impossible to understand. I was sure he had mean-looking eyes behind his reflective sunglasses—"evil eyes." I didn't trust him at all. "Wait outside, children," Mr. Willy-Bones said, "I won't be long."

Single file we shuffled back out. What was so secret?

Wil scowled. "Thought you said this Bones dude was friendly."

"He is, most of the time." Slipping my pack from my shoulders, I sank to the curb, in the shade of a parked Thunderbird. "Maybe this Evil Eyes said something to worry him."

Denise fluffed her bangs. "Characters who wear reflective sunglasses are invariably untrustworthy."

"Uh-oh!" Wil grinned and counted on his fingers. "Suspect number—four."

Five, I thought, if you counted Shirlee. Trying to put that idea out of my mind, I spoke quickly. "Denise is right, Wil. Evil Eyes does look creepy. I just hope he's not the one buying Ringo."

Denise settled on the curb beside me. "Impossible, M.D.K. *You* are buying Ringo—with the reward money!" Then, clapping her hands, she jumped up again. "How *spectacular*! If we really *can* catch the smugglers ourselves."

I looked up at Wil. "If the Parrot Man and Jerome are one and the same—what about Shirlee? She was talking to Jerome last night. Do you think she's involved?"

"Naw! Ol' Shirlee's no smuggler."

If only he was right! I wished he would stay and reassure me further. But already he was strolling around the parked Thunderbird, whistling through his teeth.

"This T-bird's a *classic*! Kinda beat up, though." Wil tried to straighten the bent antenna. "But give it a little polish—"

"When Floyd was into restoring antique cars," Denise said, "he owned a Thunderbird."

The door of the pet shop flew open, and Evil Eyes came

out. He stopped to light a cigarette, then threw down the matchbook. I was sure he was glaring at me from behind those glasses.

"Move it, kid," he ordered, waving me away from the curb.

I jumped to my feet. "Litterbug," I muttered, and scooped up the matchbook.

Stuffing it into my jeans pocket, I gave Evil Eyes a dirty look. He ignored me, climbed into the Thunderbird, and roared off. He ran a red light, turned left onto Sunset Boulevard, and sped north.

"Hope you get a ticket," I yelled after him. But wouldn't you know—Patty, our town's patrolperson, was nowhere in sight.

When we trooped back into the pet shop, Mr. Willy-Bones was hanging up the phone. "That man," I blurted. "He's not buying my parakeet—is he?"

"No," the shopkeeper said. His voice still didn't sound friendly. "He's selling birds, not buying them."

"What kind of birds?" I asked, taking the envelope from my pack. "Parrots?"

Mr. Willy-Bones scowled. "Why do you ask?"

Denise moved closer. "Because if those birds he has to sell are smuggled, we—"

"Children. My business is *my* business. And chasing the smugglers is no concern of yours either."

Wil faced Mr. Willy-Bones. "Seems if that dude broke the law, he should be arrested."

I was glad Wil stood up to Mr. Willy-Bones like that, because Wil was right!

The shopkeeper drew himself up taller. "Selling birds is only illegal if the babies come from a place where their export is prohibited. . . . I keep close contact with the Fish and Wildlife Service. If anything happens, I will notify—"

I broke in. "But Mr. Willy-Bones! We may have found one of the smugglers." I held up the envelope.

"And incriminating evidence!" Denise shouted, waving her feather.

"There's this guy by the cliffs, with a telescope," explained Wil. "He—"

"What we conclude," said Denise, "is that he spots shipments of contraband coming in—"

"A telescope? Many people have telescopes. Maybe 'this guy' likes to look at the ocean," said Mr. Willy-Bones. "I like to look at the ocean too. Does that make me a smuggler?"

Denise gave him a disgusted look, jammed the feather in her pocket, and stomped off.

I thrust the envelope under the shopkeeper's nose. "The man also gets letters from Brazil—where illegal baby parrots come from!"

Mr. Willy-Bones pulled his wire spectacles from his vest pocket. Slowly he wiped each lens with his pocket hankerchief. Then, propping the glasses on his nose, he studied the envelope.

"Foreign stamps mean nothing."

He look more closely and saw who the envelope was addressed to. He waved it away. "Nonsense. I know Jerome for thirty years. The first time I swim in the Pacific Ocean, he is the lifeguard. Perhaps this friend in Brazil is . . . who knows? . . . a friend from his lifeguarding days."

The Parrot Man—a *lifeguard*? It was hard to imagine *him* saving people's lives. I wondered if he had been as crabby then.

"I assure you," Mr. Willy-Bones said, "Jerome is no smuggler."

Wil sniffed. "Cowboys' bumpers! Something's burning!"

"*Ay!* My coffee! It bubbles over."

Mr. Willy-Bones grabbed the handle of the blue enamel pot, screamed "*Ay!*" again, and dropped it. The pot clattered onto the floor. Coffee splashed everywhere. Waving his arms, the shopkeeper shooed us away. "Out, out!" he yelled, his face flaming. "Out!"

I'd never seen him so mad. We barreled from the shop.

Outside again, Wil's face twisted into a mournful look. "M.D.K.! You forgot to introduce me to Dingo."

That made me laugh. "Let's wait till Mr. Willy-Bones isn't so cross."

Denise rolled her eyes. "I *told* you: That proprietor is a suspicious character."

Wil looked down at her. "So we're back to Suspect Number One?"

"It is obvious," she said. "He and Jerome are collaborators."

"Denise," I said, "how can you accuse dear, sweet Mr. Willy-Bones?"

"His reluctance to accuse Jerome." Denise waved her feather as she listed her reasons. "They way he puts us off when we talk about the smugglers." She looked up at Wil. "When M.D.K. and I came in here earlier, he said that we shouldn't get involved, that it wasn't our concern."

"I can't see why Mr. Willy-Bones would put up that reward poster if *he* is the smuggler," I said.

"A smoke screen," Denise said. "To throw everyone off. And did you know that your 'dear, sweet Mr. Willy-Bones' *also* corresponds with someone in Brazil?"

I was shocked. "Denise! Did you go through his *mail*?"

"Of course not. The letter was on his counter."

I shrugged. "Maybe it was to order something. . . . Brazilian-leather doggy bones . . . or leashes.''

Drat! That reminded me. *Again* I forgot to get a leash for Hilda.

Wil hooked his thumbs in his belt loops and stuck out his chest. Except for the cutoffs he looked like his dad. "What I think we oughta do is drop ol' Jerome and Mr. Willy-Nilly for now. And trail that guy with the T-bird—seeing as how he talked about selling birds."

"Perhaps illegally," Denise added, looking solemn.

"But all we know is that he drove north on Sunset," I said. "How can we follow? Run along behind his car?"

"We could go by bus," Denise said. "If we knew his destination."

"Wait—maybe we do." I reached into the pocket of my jeans for the matchbook. "He dropped this."

Before I could read the words on the cover, Denise grabbed it. Her eyes bugged. "*Incredible!* An ad for Sam's Oyster Bar."

Wil whistled. "Isn't that where Jerome and Shirlee were headed—the place on Malibu Pier?"

Denise nodded.

"What're we waiting for?" Wil asked. "Let's go to Malibu."

Denise waved her arms and skipped in circles. "Floyd is gone, so the beach house is empty. It can serve as our lookout. I will run home and get the key."

"Wait, you two!" I shouted. "I still have pets to feed. And what about bus fare? Who has money?"

Denise shook her head.

"I have just enough to get back to Santa Monica tonight," Wil said.

Drat! I chewed my thumbnail, thinking. Then I remembered Mrs. Kenilworth. "Puddy's mom owes me money. I'll collect it when I go up there." I pulled a bunch of carrot tops from my pack. "Can you take these greens to Bun?"

"Sure. Where's he live?"

After I gave Wil instructions, the three of us took off in different directions. We agreed to meet at the bus stop on the corner of Ocean and Sunset.

When I arrived there, twenty minutes later, Wil was waiting alone.

He grinned. "Fed ol' Bun! What'd the kid say about your switching fish on him?"

"Never knew the difference. Not only that, but his mom liked the new fish so much, she gave me a tip!" I waved two five-dollar bills. "And she says she might start raising tropicals."

Denise raced toward us. "Sustenance!" she yelled, holding high a paper bag. "Muffins and apples for lunch.

"And, M.D.K.," she added when she got closer, "you will never believe who I saw entering the pet shop just now."

"Who?"

"Shirlee Alabama."

"Sure, Denise." I sighed. "Sure you did."

9

Spies on the Pier

I WAS FIRST ONTO THE CROWDED BUS. HANDING THE driver one of the fives from Mrs. Kenilworth, I said, "For me and my two friends."

Wouldn't you know? The minute Denise stepped on, she dropped the paper bag. Everything spilled. The muffins were squashed, but we recovered the apples. Wil wiped off his and began chomping on it while working his way to the back. He had to stand all the way to Malibu. Denise and I were luckier. We found empty seats. Mine was next to a woman and a fussy baby who kept pulling my hair. Munching my bruised apple, I puzzled over the connection between Shirlee and Mr. Willy-Bones.

Finally I gave up. Shirlee's friendship with the Parrot Man was mystery enough. For them to meet at Malibu Pier didn't make sense. Why were they there? Did they go into Sam's Oyster Bar to meet Evil Eyes Perry? More questions than answers swam around in my head.

Wil must have done some thinking on the ride too. When we hopped off, he announced, "I bet Shirlee and her birdman sweetie aren't even smugglers. They're after the reward money—same as us."

My jaw dropped. For a minute I was too stunned to answer. Then I asked Wil, "So who *are* the smugglers?"

"It's gotta be that Evil Eyes Perry," he said.

After we crossed the highway to the beach side, Denise was still sputtering. "But . . . but . . . the broken crates from Mexico. The letter. . . . The feather. You mean all our evidence is *inconclusive*?"

"My hunch is ol' Jerome keeps track of Evil Eyes with that telescope," Wil said. "Today he saw something suspicious. So he went up to check. Shirlee came with him."

Usually Wil's hunches proved to be right, but I wasn't sure about this one. "What about the semaphore signals?" I asked.

"Perhaps Jerome and Shirlee have an accomplice," Denise said.

"Only bad guys have accomplices," I told her.

Denise smiled sweetly. "Not necessarily. That is the usual interpretation of 'accomplice.' But it can also be defined as an associate in *any* undertaking."

Quickly I changed the subject. "I'm starved. Let's start with lunch at Sam's Oyster Bar. My treat—courtesy of Mrs. Kenilworth."

Wil's forehead wrinkled. "Don't cotton much to oysters."

"It is a varied menu," Denise said. "They serve other foods, such as clam sandwiches. We can have dessert at the beach house. Floyd always keeps *cartons* of orange Popsicles in the freezer."

We headed for Sam's, a wooden shack close to the highway at the entrance of Malibu Pier. Wil sniffed as we stepped onto the pier. "That salt air sure smells good." Then he grinned. "Can't wait to go swimming."

"Swimming?" I said.

"No time for frivolity," Denise added. "We must search out that scofflaw."

"Just kidding." Wil jumped aside to avoid a kid zooming by on a skateboard, then followed us into Sam's. He zeroed in on a redwood picnic table by the window. "How about sitting here? I can watch the surfers while we eat."

We were the only customers. The young man at the oyster bar seemed to be the only waiter. He put down his curved oyster-shucking knife, wiped both hands on his striped apron, and ambled over to take our order.

"Are clam sandwiches on sourdough satisfactory?" Denise looked at Wil and me. He shrugged like he was still unsure, but I nodded.

"Three clam sours," she told the waiter.

"And Tim," she added. "Three glasses of water—with ice."

"You *know* him?" I asked when the waiter was gone.

She nodded. "He has worked here for a couple of years."

"So ask him about Evil Eyes," I said.

When he brought our sandwiches, Denise asked, "Tim, do any of your customers drive an old green Thunderbird?"

He scowled. "Jeez, Denny. How should I know what cars people drive?" But when he had settled onto his stool at the oyster bar, he called over. "The waiter who comes on duty at four used to work in the parking lot—he might know."

"So we sit here till *then*?" I asked Denise.

"We can wait at the beach house," she said. "Sam's is visible from our patio. We can eat Popsicles and watch."

After taking one bite, Wil put down his sandwich. He gazed at the menu chalked on a blackboard behind the oyster bar. Then he hooted. "Tex-Mex chili! Cowboys' bumpers, wish I'd known."

Denise nodded. "Sam's cook is *perpetually* experimenting."

"Maybe that's why ol' Shirlee stopped by. For a taste o' home."

"You'd think she'd get enough at my house," I said.

Wil scraped all the clams left in his sandwich onto his plate. Then he stuffed the bread in his mouth and slid from the booth. "Meet y'all out front," he said, heading for the door.

"Where did he disappear to?" Denise asked.

"Bathroom, maybe?"

She shook her head. "The rest rooms are in the other direction."

We quickly finished our food, and I paid the waiter with the other five-dollar bill from Mrs. Kenilworth. Then we went out into the sunshine. Wil hurried to meet us.

"Had a hunch," he said, tugging his earlobe. "Figured maybe that kid on the skateboard might know something. Chased him down. Asked if he'd seen a skinny guy with an old green T-bird." A big smile spread across Wil's freckled face. "The kid knows that guy! Sees him hanging around Sam's all the time."

"So Tim was lying," said Denise.

"Or never noticed," I said.

Wil leaned over the wooden railing to look at cars in the parking lot below. "No classic T-birds there now. We'll have to wait till ol' Evil Eyes turns up."

Denise waved her feather. "Then we follow him—"

"And he leads us to the rest of his gang!" I shouted.

Wil nodded toward the far end of the pier. "While we're waiting, how about we walk clear out on the pier. So I can look down on the *bee-oo-ti-ful* blue Pacific."

He loped ahead. Denise and I followed. From both sides of the pier old people and kids dangled their fishing lines in the water below. Not many caught fish, but everyone looked happy. We lost sight of Wil when a crowd of laughing, joking people rushed past us, carrying bulging gunnysacks.

"Day-trippers with their day's catch," explained Denise. "They debarked from that fishing boat docked at the end of the pier."

"Those sacks are a good way to sneak baby birds ashore," I remarked.

Denise nodded. "My thoughts precisely."

"Wonder what they'd do," I said, "if we asked to look inside the sacks?"

At the end of the pier, Wil, cheerful as usual, was talking with two leathery-faced men in watch caps who were busy cutting bait. They looked like they were having fun. Denise tugged my arm. In a loud whisper she said, "Those characters look *highly* suspicious."

I giggled and ran to Wil, but I didn't waste time reporting Denise's latest suspects. "We should head back soon. We don't want to miss—"

One of the grizzled bait-cutters stopped work to listen. I hesitated. Maybe Denise was right. To be safe, I quit talking.

Wil knew what I meant. He nodded. Our feet thumping on the wooden pier, we raced back toward the Coast Highway. After we passed Sam's, Denise pointed south with her feather. "Our beach house is down that road."

She led us along a gravel road between the highway and the back fences of the beach houses. The high fences of wood or stucco blocked our view of the sand, but sometimes, even over the traffic noise of the Coast Highway, we could hear the surf.

Denise stopped at a fence of weathered redwood and unlocked a door. "This is it." We followed her into a two-car garage. Now the only car was Floyd's white Mercedes. Boxes, a bicycle, and stacks of life jackets lined the front wall. Though the bright orange jackets looked new, two were so ripped that the kapok stuffing hung out. I wondered how they had gotten torn. One thing for sure:

Wearing one of those wouldn't keep you afloat for two seconds!

We stepped into the small backyard. Wil pointed to four surfboards leaning against a wall. He gave a low whistle. "Cowabunga! Do you do that much surfing?"

Denise made a face. "Not me. Floyd. He and his aging friends have this dream that they are still hotshot surfers."

On the north side, between the beach house and the neighbor's high stone fence, was a gate.

"Where does that go?" I asked.

"Shortcut to the front. But we will go through the house." Denise unlocked the back door. We followed her through the kitchen and dining area and into the living room. The front wall was solid glass, with floor-to-ceiling windows and a sliding glass door.

Wil whistled. "Look at that. Right out there's the ocean." He grinned. "Bet you come here a lot."

Denise shook her head. "This is where Floyd always meets with his crones—and he hates having me around."

"Meets about what?" Wil asked. "Surfing?"

"Who knows? Ever since *Kiddie Brigade* went into reruns, Floyd has been trying to make a TV comeback. He is *perpetually* concocting some new scheme to make money."

That surprised me. I had this notion that TV stars—even has-beens like Floyd—had more money than they knew what to do with.

"From the patio we can see Sam's." Denise unlocked the sliding glass door. "Go on out. I will bring the Popsicles."

"None for me," Wil said, pointing to kids skimming the surf on Styrofoam kickboards. "Y'all watch for ol' Evil Eyes. I'll be back." With a wild Texas "Yahoo!" he was gone.

He was already splashing in the surf by the time I threw

down my pack and settled into a yellow-canvas director's chair on the patio.

Denise came out, a frown on her face. "For some weird reason, not a *single* Popsicle in the freezer." She handed me a plastic tumbler. "Have some water."

After one sip, I set the tumbler on the glass-topped table. Yuck! The water was lukewarm.

Denise handed me a copy of *Animals in the Wild*. "Here is the magazine I was telling you about. Floyd must have brought it up yesterday. The article on smuggling is on page twenty-three."

She leaned over my shoulder and pointed. "Here it describes how the poachers reach the parrots' nests."

I squirmed away. "Denise! Just 'cause I don't get straight *A's* in reading like you doesn't mean I don't know how."

"Sorry! But can you *believe*? They chop down an entire tree." She still hovered over me. "They destroy the parrots' nesting place *forever*—merely because it makes collecting the birds simpler." She waved an arm. "Here it shows—"

"Denise!" I shouted.

Too late! Her elbow bumped the tumbler. Water splashed my hand, and I dropped the magazine.

"Sorry!" she cried.

I picked up the soggy magazine. "It's soaked."

"Never mind. Just leave it on the table to dry."

"Hey, you two!" Wil charged through the sand toward us. "Guess what that Old Geezer was doing?"

"Geezer?" I stared at him.

"That bait cutter. The one I talked to, on the pier. He has semaphore flags, like Jerome's . . . and he was sending signals."

I gasped. "Who to? The smugglers?"

Denise danced around, kicking up sand and clapping

her hands. "I *knew* it . . . I *told* you that bait cutter looked suspicious. This proves it."

I pulled my sketchbook and a colored pencil from my pack to write down important clues.

"Where was he signaling?" I asked Wil.

He pointed south. "That way—toward Pacific Cliffs."

"The Parrot Man!" I drew in my breath.

"Can you decipher semaphore?" Denise asked Wil. "What was the message?"

"I can read it—sort of. But it doesn't matter, anyhow. By the time I figured what was happening, the Geezer'd stopped. But my hunch is that he's Jerome's lookout."

"So *he* is the accomplice of Jerome and Shirlee," Denise said. "Which means he is also in pursuit of the lawbreakers."

Wil frowned. "Unless . . ."

I studied his wrinkled forehead. Was he having second thoughts about Shirlee and the Parrot Man too? Then the creases vanished and Wil grinned. "*Naw!* No way could ol' Shirlee be a smuggler's moll."

Denise fiddled with her feather. "One thing is obvious. The pier is their headquarters."

Wil looked up from tying his sneakers. "Or maybe Sam's Oyster Bar."

"I'm calling Mr. Willy-Bones," I announced. "He'll be mad about what we're doing—but I don't care. He might know who this Old Geezer is. And I think it's time for him to call the Fish and Wildlife Service."

"Can you trust him?" Denise asked.

"We have to. What else can we do?" I looked back toward the oyster bar. "This is dumb. We were supposed to be watching for Evil Eyes. By now he could have come—and gone again."

"Let us check the parking lot by Sam's," said Denise.

We went inside, and she locked the sliding glass door at the front. We left the beach house the way we entered.

"Shouldn't we sweep up?" I asked. Our gritty trails of sand stretched clear through the house.

Denise shrugged. "Let Floyd. It will be even messier when he returns from his fishing trip and unloads all his gear."

As we walked back to Sam's, Denise apologized about the mix-up with the Popsicles. "But there is a snow-cone stand on the pier," she said.

I shook my head. "It must be nearly five, and I've got to be home by six."

Denise stopped twirling her feather long enough to consult her Swatch watch. "Four fifty-four, to be precise."

"In that case forget the snow cones *and* Evil Eyes."

"Come on, M.D.K.," Wil protested. "Just a quick look into the parking lot."

We lucked out. Denise hurried across the wooden pier ahead of us and let out a squeal. She pointed with her feather at the parking lot below. Two men stood next to the green Thunderbird. I had never seen the lunky one with the bumpy complexion before. But I recognized the tall, thin man in the flowered Hawaiian shirt. It was Evil Eyes.

"Get down," Wil ordered in a low voice. "And keep quiet." After dropping onto our stomachs, we inched toward the edge of the wooden pier until we could peek over. It was the perfect place to spy. From below, the words of the two men drifted up.

"Message just came . . . ship-to-shore radio," Evil Eyes said. "The boat's due on Friday . . . about twelve."

"How many birds?" the lunky man asked.

"Dunno. . . . Transmission was garbled—"

"Oops!" Denise shrieked as her feather floated down toward the men. Evil Eyes spun around.

"Who's up there?" he demanded, shaking his fist.

10

The Promise

WE FLATTENED OURSELVES ON THE ROUGH WOODEN pier. Nobody breathed. Nobody moved. We had drawn back from the edge the instant Denise had let out that shriek. Evil Eyes hadn't seen us—I was almost sure. I found a crack between two boards wide enough to peek down at the two men. Evil Eyes was looking all around. He seemed puzzled by Denise's yelp.

"Forget it," his friend with the lumpy face said. "Just some wiseacre kids."

Still Evil Eyes glowered up at the underside of the pier.

"C'mon, Ernie," Lump Face urged. "Let's go have a beer."

The two men finally moved off. We scrambled to our feet as soon as they hurried up the incline and disappeared inside Sam's.

Denise peered down at the parking lot. "I must retrieve my feather. It could be vital evidence."

"You'd never find it," Wil said.

"And anyway," I shouted, sprinting toward the Coast Highway, "here comes our bus."

Reluctantly Denise raced after Wil and me. We reached the stop at the same instant the southbound bus did. This time we found three seats together at the back. Wil sat in the middle.

"I'm still in shock," I said. "They really *are* smuggling birds!"

"Undoubtedly," Denise said, her eyes round as beach balls. "That Ernie 'Evil Eyes' Perry is *sinister!*"

"And so is his friend Lump Face," I said.

Wil nodded. "Had a hunch those guys'd come by boat."

"So all we have to do," I said, "is be there when they dock at twelve—"

"At night!" Denise interrupted. "Obviously such underworld types operate after dark. Less danger of detection."

"If it's midnight, forget it," I said. "Shirlee will never let me go up there that late."

"Unless she is there herself," Denise said.

"Could be that's what the Old Geezer was signaling to Jerome." Wil shifted in his seat. "I wonder how much those two old guys and Shirlee know. Maybe we should join forces."

"And let them claim the reward?" Denise snorted. "Forget *that*. M.D.K. needs enough money to buy her parakeet."

"Doesn't matter," I said. "We can't worry about Ringo now. All I want is to nab those smugglers." I stared out the window as the bus rumbled down the Coast Highway. I couldn't believe I'd just said that. But once the words tumbled out, I realized that that was how I felt. More important than the reward was stopping those evil men before they harmed any more poor birds.

Wil smiled at me. "Don't worry, M.D.K.—you'll get ol' Bingo."

"Maybe," I said. Then quickly I added, "But Friday's the day after tomorrow. If that's when their smuggled birds get here, we haven't much time." I reached into my pack, on the floor at my feet, and brought out my sketchbook. "We'd better start planning."

"Right, Detective Kincaid." Wil gave me a salute. "So first we figure *when* and *where* the smugglers are due to arrive—"

"And where they go afterward," said Denise. "Undoubtedly they will try to foist their illegal birds on several pet shops."

"Which reminds me," Wil said. "M.D.K., you were going to give your old friend Mr. W.B. a call."

Drat! I knocked my fist on my forehead. "I meant to phone Mr. Willy-Bones from the beach house. And I forgot."

"By the time we get back, he will be closed," Denise said.

I nodded. "I'll go and see him first thing in the morning."

"Do it by phone," Wil said. "You should stick with Shirlee tomorrow. Like *glue*. We need to know what she's up to."

"Now," he said, sitting straighter in the seat. "For our plan of action." Sometimes Wil acted goofy, but he was better than me at getting organized. "Notebook ready, Detective Kincaid?"

"Ready." I waved a red drawing pencil.

"Better hurry," Denise said as the bus turned to begin to climb toward Pacific Cliffs. "We are practically home."

"Right," Wil said. He scratched his head. "Denise, can you trail the Parrot Man tomorrow?"

"I can only keep him under surveillance until ten," she said. "Then I have an optometrist's appointment."

"It'll have to do." Wil wrinkled his freckled nose. "And I'll chase after the Geezer and Evil Eyes. And this new dude, Lump Face."

"If I have to stay home all day," I said, "who's going to take care of the rabbit and the tortoise and—"

"Maybe Wil can stop off on his way to Malibu," Denise said.

Wil nodded. "Sure. Stuffing lettuce in a cage is no big deal."

"Before my appointment, I will have time to care for Hilda and Conrad," Denise said.

"Can you take care of the canaries, too?" I asked her.

"Do I have to?"

"If I stay with Shirlee all day, I don't see how—"

Wil broke in. "Never mind. Let me do it. I like birds."

Good old Wil. Always the peacemaker.

"It is not a matter of *like* or *dislike*," Denise said. "I absolutely *abhor* seeing wild birds caged."

"Canaries aren't wild birds," I said. "And they're better off in cages than out where a dumb cat can eat them."

Denise scowled. "Cats are not dumb."

I scowled back. "They can't talk, can they?"

"Neither can birds," Denise said. "Mimicking is not the same as actually talking."

My whole body tensed up. I stared from the bus window, counting to ten. Sometimes Denise really teed me off. Why did she have to rub it in about Ringo and caged birds?

"You *guys*!" Wil yelled. "This is your stop."

I stuffed my notebook into my pack. With Denise at my heels I raced for the door. "Call you tonight," I shouted to Wil as we hopped off. I could give him instructions for the pets then.

As soon as the bus pulled away, I turned to Denise. I smiled. She had been a big help. Her feelings about caged birds were no reason to fight. "Thanks for all the help pet-sitting," I said.

"Sure." She smiled too. "And just remember, when

you ferret information from your sitter, be casual. The operative words are nonchalant, noncommital, and disinterested.''

"I'll try.''

"By the way,'' Denise said. "Do you recall that tabby that was by my house the other day? She returned. I have been feeding her.''

"What about Floyd's allergy?''

She grinned. "I will let him worry about that when he gets back.''

We parted at the corner with a wave. All the way to the top of my hill I practiced being casual, nonchalant, noncommital, and disinterested. Not easy, considering I was excited, curious, and highly suspicious—of Shirlee Alabama.

"Hi, I'm home!'' I shouted, bounding into the house. The usual smell of chili greeted me. After a week I was used to it.

"Lordy, Miss Margaret!'' Shirlee marched from the kitchen, strings flapping on her checkered apron. "It's nearly seven. I been worried sick. . . . If your mama only knew—''

"Sorry I'm late.'' I gave her a smile I hoped was casual. "We were in Malibu, and the bus—''

"Malibu?" she screeched. Her red eyebrows formed an angry V. "Why on earth were you up there?''

"Denise invited us . . . to her beach house.'' Drat! This whole thing was going backward. *I* was supposed to be the one asking questions. Before Shirlee could ask anything more, I gave her a nonchalant smile. "Any phone messages? Did my folks call?''

"Mail's on the hall table,'' she snapped, and stormed back to the kitchen.

I dropped my pack. First I read Mom's postcard, mailed from Redding, a town in Northern California. She was fine. She had another week and a half of flying her politician around the state, and then she'd be home. She would try to call me on Friday.

Friday! That reminded me of my assignment to "ferret information," as Denise put it. Shoving the letter from Dad into my pocket to read later, I hurried into the kitchen. I tried a noncommital smile. Shirlee was too busy at the stove to catch it.

"So how was your day?" That seemed disinterested enough.

She swiped a bony hand across her forehead. "Not bad, considerin' I was over a hot stove since the crack o' dawn."

"But isn't Wednesday your day at the Senior Center?" I tried to pretend it was a casual question and that I really couldn't care less.

Shirlee's cheeks turned redder under the rouge spots. "Well, I did run over to the Center for a half hour or so. Then I had to get back to fix your supper."

I stared at the chili bubbling in that pot. Why cook more? Already dozens of jars of the stuff jammed the fridge. What I *ought* to ask Shirlee was: Why so much Tex-Mex?

"Didn't count on your gettin' back this late." She clucked and stirred. "Not safe . . . a young girl like you . . . out at all hours."

I gave up trying to quiz her and pulled out Dad's letter to read. He was fine, same as Mom. He had a week or more of business to finish up and he might not get home until Labor Day.

"Supper's ready," Shirlee squawked.

Stuffing Dad's letter into my pocket, I started to sit down. Then I remembered my dirty hands. After I washed them at the sink, I slipped into my chair at the kitchen table, gave Shirlee another noncommital smile, and began to eat.

When the phone rang, we both leaped up. We nearly collided. Shirlee got to it first. All she said was "Yes," "No," and "Mebbe" between long silences. Finally I gave up listening and went back to eating. Suddenly she cackled.

"Yer dern-tootin' I'll be ready. Just see that you have that van here on time," she said, and hung up.

When she came back to the table, I shrugged my shoulders. Nonchalantly.

"Good news?"

Shirlee didn't answer. She only jammed a loose hairpin firmly into her topknot and cleared the table. Soon she set before me a huge slice of gingerbread. It was still warm from the oven and smelled heavenly. I was suspicious. Except for occasional baked apples Shirlee *never* gave me dessert. Now two nights in a row she had plied me with goodies.

"Baked it myself!" she crowed, smiling proudly.

"Yummy," I said, diving in. It looked an awful lot like Sara Lee, but how could I be sure? Between bites, I searched for telltale bits of plastic wrap, but couldn't find any.

Shirlee looked down her thin nose at me. "So what did you do in Malibu, Miss Margaret?"

Her question was so unexpected, I nearly choked.

"Goofed around." I stared at my plate. "Showed Wil the beach."

"You didn't talk to any strangers?" she demanded.

"Never do!" I knew better than that.

Leaning an elbow on the table, she waved a bony finger. "See that you don't. . . . There's unsavory types about . . . purse snatchers, bird smugglers—"

My head jerked up. "Bird smugglers?"

"So I hear. At the Center my friend was sayin'—" She suddenly returned to the stove and began stirring the pot on it. "Never mind. But I don't want you gallivantin' after smugglers, like you did down in Texas."

I didn't say anything. I didn't know what to say.

" 'Cause I won't have it, you hear?" She waved her wooden spoon at me. "Don't want you mixed up with people like *that* . . . so don't get it in your head to go lookin' for 'em—"

"I . . . won't." I felt my cheeks burning.

"Do you promise, Miss Margaret?"

"I . . . I promise," I said.

11

The Message in the Margin

EVEN WITH MY HAND UNDER THE TABLE AND MY FIN-
gers crossed, I felt bad about lying to Shirlee. But Denise
and Wil and I were in this too deep. We'd found the smugglers—some of them anyway. We knew their plans. If we
stopped now, they might get away with their evil deed.

Shirlee returned to her pot of chili. I got up and went
into the living room.

"Where's the *TV Guide*?" I shouted. "It's not on the
set, where it's s'posed to be."

"Mighta left it in the den," Shirlee called.

She didn't say "don't go in," so I figured she wouldn't
mind. Being there felt strange. It was the first time I'd
gone into the den since Shirlee had taken it over as her
room. Pink hair curlers and wads of Kleenex cluttered the
top of Dad's oak desk. Her pink chenille robe was draped
across the back of Mom's antique rocking chair.

The program guide lay under a jar of cold cream on the
desk. Flipping through the guide, I saw a note in the margin in Shirlee's handwriting: *Del. B.P. Friday, 12:00.* But
what did it mean?

The day and the time grabbed my attention. Twelve on
Friday was when Evil Eyes expected that big delivery. Did

this note mean Shirlee was a part of the smuggling ring after all?

After ripping off the corner of the page with her writing, I rushed from the den. Wil should know about this *right now*! So should Denise. But when I got to the kitchen, Shirlee was still fussing at the counter. With her there I couldn't call anybody. She was sifting flour. From the smell of spices I could tell she was about to bake more gingerbread. Chili beans boiled on the stove. What was she planning—a welcome-home party for the smugglers?

I went to my room and noted this latest clue in my sketchbook. Afterward I tried reading a mystery, but every few minutes I got up to check if it was safe to call my friends. At last I heard the TV set blaring. Good! Shirlee was finally out of the kitchen.

Sneaking to the phone, I tried to reach Denise, but there was no answer. I held my breath and dialed another number. "Hello?" Wil answered on the first ring. Breathlessly I told him about the note in the *TV Guide*.

"Aha! Detective Kincaid uncovers the Mysterious Message in the Margin."

"Be serious, Wil. This could be important." I kept my voice low. "The 'Del' must mean 'delivery' . . . but I can't figure out 'B.P.' "

"Beats me," Wil said. "The initials of a friend, maybe?"

"Jerome, the Parrot Man, is her only friend that I know about," I said. "But she did talk to somebody on the phone during dinner about a van. What can that mean?"

"Maybe 'B.P.' stands for 'ball park.' Could be that a van is hauling Shirlee and her Senior Center buddies to a doubleheader!"

"There's no ball game around here on Friday, Wil."

If only Denise were home. She'd figure it out right away.

Then Wil laughed. "What about 'big pizza'? Maybe she's having one delivered for your lunch on Friday."

"Don't I wish!" But this was no time to clown. Why couldn't Wil be serious?

"Wait," Wil said. "I have it! Remember that beauty shop a few doors down from Billy-Boy's pet shop? It's spelled like *D e l . . .* something."

"Delia's?" I gasped. Sometimes that goofy Wil really surprised me. "Wil, you're a genius. That's *it*! Delia's Beauty Parlor!—'Del. B.P.' I'll bet Shirlee made an appointment to get her hair dyed." I giggled. "It's about time. The gray roots are starting to show."

The explanation made sense. And although the van was still a mystery, I was relieved. It didn't look like Shirlee was part of the smuggling ring after all.

"Another thing, Wil. Shirlee says there's talk at the Center about smugglers in the area. She made me promise not to get involved."

"You mean you want to back out?"

"We can't back out now, Wil. But I can't let Shirlee find out. She'd *kill* me."

"You can count on me, M.D.K. I'll never squeal."

After giving Wil directions for feeding Bun and the tortoise, I hung up. When I passed the living room, Shirlee was asleep in the E-Z lounger. Her snoring was louder than the blaring TV set. I tiptoed to my room, slipped on my nightie, and popped into bed.

When the phone jangled, I bolted upright, instantly awake. Had something happened to Mom or Dad? I jumped from bed, not sure how long I had been sleeping. It felt like the middle of the night. I groped down the hall.

In the kitchen the light was on. Hearing Shirlee's voice, I stopped to listen.

"Why, Jerome. I was just a-fixin' to call you. . . ."

So it wasn't Mom or Dad in trouble. *That* was a relief! I remained in the shadows, listening. The clock struck twelve. Why a call from the Parrot Man at this hour?

". . . So is it all set for Friday?" Shirlee was asking. "And you can borrow the van?"

The van again! So the phone call earlier must have been from Jerome too. But what did the van have to do with her appointment at the beauty parlor?

Shirlee clucked. "Stop fussin', Jerome. It'll go without a hitch. . . ."

What would? Her appointment at Delia's? For gosh sakes! Dying hair wasn't *that* risky. And what was Jerome—her chauffeur?

Or maybe his bad-tempered parrot was having its feathers dyed. I almost giggled out loud.

"The only thing worryin' me," Shirlee said, "is four deliveries in one day. Besides the two in Malibu, we've got the one here in town . . . and Santa Monica besides. Think we oughta leave Santa Monica till Saturday?"

She said nothing more except "Good night" before setting down the receiver. I tore back down the hall to my room.

Lying in the dark, I puzzled over Shirlee's conversation. "Del. B.P." did *not* stand for Delia's Beauty Parlor, of that I was certain. Now I was sure that "Del" stood for delivery, just like I'd thought at first. And whatever Shirlee planned to do Friday at twelve, Jerome and his van were involved in it too. Maybe the Old Geezer, as well.

So what was "B.P." Bean Pot? Bad Penny? The clock chimed one. Still I couldn't figure out what the initials meant. Was it Baked Potato? Blue Pencil? Not being able to solve what could be the key to this whole mystery was a *Big Pain*! What kind of detective was I, anyway?

I thought about trying one more time to call Denise. But what if Shirlee heard me? So instead I got up, switched

on my bed lamp, and opened my dictionary. I would un-
scramble that message if I had to go through every page
of *B*s and every page of *P*s.

On the first page of the *B*s I broke the code. *Baby!* What
a dumbo. I should have guessed right away. And the second word *had* to be *Parrots*. This proved Shirlee and Jerome knew about the smuggling operation. But did that
mean they were part of it? Was all that chili for feeding
the rest of her gang?

Sharing my house with a smuggler scared me. It was
spooky. But it was too late to make any more calls. Nothing could be done until morning.

Nothing, that is, except barricade my room.

I shoved a sturdy toy chest against my door. It was one
Dad had built of thick mahogany planks when I was a
mini-kid. I loaded the chest with every heavy object I
owned—books, shoes, a lamp, my paint box, my stamp
collection, even my flute in its leather case. For good mea-
sure I tossed my beanbag chair on top.

If Shirlee tried to push past all that, I would have loads
of time to escape through the window.

12

A Crisis!

I DREAMED OF BABY PARROTS. POACHERS SNATCHED them from their jungle nests, stuffed them into nylon panty hose, crammed them under car seats and in spare tires. The poor birds were smuggled across borders—their tiny beaks taped so they couldn't make a sound. It was horrible. I kept waking up, only to fall asleep and dream again of helpless baby parrots and evil smugglers.

In the morning I leaped from my bed to phone Wil. Then I came up against that barricade. Drat! Removing enough junk to budge the toy chest took so long that when I finally got free and raced for the kitchen, Shirlee was already up and cooking breakfast. So much for calling Wil.

"French toast this morning, sweetie?" Shirlee gave me a wide smile showing all of her gold fillings.

"No, thanks." Any other time my mouth would have watered at the good smell of butter sizzling in the skillet. But how could I eat food cooked by a smuggler's moll?

I poured myself a bowl of Cheerios and studied Shirlee's wrinkled cheeks, still pale before her daily coating of rouge. How had this old lady from Texas gotten mixed up with smugglers? Jerome's doing, probably. She had met him—it didn't matter where—and he had lured her into joining his smuggling ring. She'd needed the money, so why not? She'd make more than she did selling Tex-Mex at her little café in Riverbank.

No wonder she didn't tell Wil and his dad why she might stay in California.

"Sure you won't try even an itty-bitty piece of French toast?" Shirlee asked, interrupting my thoughts.

Shaking my head, I swallowed another spoonful of Cheerios. They didn't make me feel cheery at all. Shirlee took the skillet to the sink. Mincing across the linoleum in her tight jeans and boots, she just didn't look or act like a criminal. She was hard to get along with sometimes— "Feisty," Mom had called her—but how could Shirlee be *that* bad?

"Aren't you s'posed to be doin' your rounds?" she asked.

"What? Oh . . . well, I—" Her question had caught me off guard. I felt my face turning red. "My friends want to do them alone for a change." It was more white lie than real fib. "So I decided to lounge around the house all day."

I had better watch my step or she might discover what we were up to. Now I knew why she'd made me promise not to go after the smugglers. It was not to keep me from getting hurt. It was to keep *her* and the others from getting caught.

I slipped my empty cereal bowl and spoon into the sudsy water in the sink and glanced up at the kitchen clock. After nine! Too late now to phone Wil. He would already be on the bus, coming up from Santa Monica to feed my pets. And Denise had that doctor's appointment. But I *could* phone Mr. Willy-Bones if Shirlee ever left the kitchen.

Although we had an electric dishwasher, Shirlee preferred to wash dishes by hand. I picked up a dish towel and started to dry the ones that were draining. Anything to speed things up.

Then the phone rang. I raced for it, but Shirlee had already grabbed it.

"And good morning to you, sweetheart," she said. "You're up bright and early. Any word from your daddy?" Shirlee practically purred. "Did he catch any fish down there in Baja?"

So it was Denise! Simpering, Shirlee handed over the receiver. "It's your little friend." In a loud whisper she added, "The one whose daddy does that TV show."

"Stepdad," I muttered, grabbing the phone.

Shirlee went back to the sink, but washed the dishes so quietly, I knew she must be listening.

"M.D.K.!" Denise shrieked. "You will never *believe*! This morning when Izzy and I went over to feed Hilda—"

"Izzy?"

"I have named that adorable tabby Isadora."

"What about Mrs. Eastley's dachshund? What happened?"

"Nothing. She is fine. But parked in front of Jerome's gate is an old van. And in addition to *that*, I saw him sending a *semaphore message*—"

Shirlee stopped washing dishes altogether.

"Not so loud," I told Denise. "You're killing my eardrums."

"I get it. You are not *alone* . . . right?" Denise lowered her voice to a husky whisper.

"Right."

"To continue. . . . I wrote down which directions the flags pointed . . . for Wil to translate." Denise's voice grew so soft, I barely understood her. But that was all right. Shirlee wouldn't be able to either.

"But I must leave *immediately* for my optometrist appointment," Denise went on. "Can you deliver this paper to Wil for me? The message could be of the *utmost* significance.''

I guess she meant ''important.'' It probably was. But how could I spy on Shirlee and get the paper to Wil, too?

''In present circumstances . . . impossible . . . to vacate premises.'' I hoped Denise understood my code.

''You mean you have to stay there and snoop?''

''Affirmative. Unexpected developments. . . .'' This was fun. For a change, I was the one using the big words. But with Shirlee listening, I didn't dare say more. ''I'll explain later.''

''I must dash anyway. My mother is sitting on the car horn,'' said Denise. ''I will leave the paper on the porch, beneath a brick—''

''Denise, I can't—''

But she had hung up. Whatever that important message was, I knew there was no way I could collect that paper.

Replacing the receiver, I noticed strange marks on the notepad by the phone. There were zigzag lines and arrows, and also letters—*MALXX, WBX, SMX.* I realized they were Shirlee's scribblings from that midnight conversation with Jerome. But the marks didn't make sense. I ripped off the sheet anyway and stuck it into my pocket. It could be an important clue. A map, maybe. Or a kind of code.

For the rest of the morning, I trailed Shirlee. It was a waste of time, though. She went through her morning routine. She sorted laundry, washed a couple of windows, vacuumed the hall. I even followed her into the backyard when she buried the garbage.

''But we've got a disposal in the kitchen,'' I said.

''A friend at the Senior Center tells me it makes flowers bloom better.''

I scratched my head. Our garden was mostly weeds,

except for Mom's geraniums. And they seemed to be doing fine on their own.

Around lunchtime Shirlee disappeared into the bathroom. I dropped the peanut-butter sandwich I was making as soon as the shower started. I raced to the phone book. There it was, the number of the pet shop. I dialed it.

Mr. Willy-Bones didn't answer. I let the phone ring three times. Then I heard his voice. Only it wasn't him. It was a recording: ". . . unable to come to the phone. . . . Leave a message . . . sound of the beep." Ugh! I *hated* answering machines. I was still trying to figure what to say when the bathroom door opened. Shirlee dashed out in her pink robe, a towel wrapped around her head. She swished by me and into the den.

I put down the receiver. I couldn't leave that message now. Not with Shirlee listening. And anyway, what I had to say was too important to trust to a dumb tape recorder. I needed to talk to Mr. Willy-Bones. Time was running out.

By early afternoon Shirlee had settled in the E-Z lounger to do her nails and watch the soaps. With her hair in curlers and her feet propped up, she looked as if she wasn't going anyplace for ages.

But I was! I had wasted far too much time already.

On a card by the phone Mom and Dad kept important numbers, such as the police, the fire department, our doctor, and the Pacific Cliffs Taxi Service. What fun to dial 911, but I didn't dare. Instead I called for a taxi.

"No, this isn't a joke," I told the man who answered. "It's an emergency. I'll be waiting at the corner of Chautauqua and Ellis streets—and I have money to pay."

I had never ridden in a taxi before, but I knew they were expensive. I rushed to my room and dumped out all the bills and coins from Sinclair, my dinosaur bank. This time I wouldn't bother with my pack. Instead I stuffed my entire savings into my jeans pocket. Whatever the cab ride cost, that should cover it.

I slipped from the house and raced to the corner. A black-and-red taxi approached and stopped. I jumped in.

"First take me to Edgecliff Estates," I told the driver. "Then to Malibu. And hurry! This is a *crisis*."

13

Caught in the Act

I RAN TO THE END OF THE PIER. WIL WASN'T THERE. I'd already checked the beach, and Sam's. Where *was* he? Then I looked toward Denise's beach house. There was Wil, lounging in a canvas chair on the front patio. He wasn't acting like there was a crisis.

I raced over. "How'd you get in without a key?" I demanded.

He laughed. "Don't need one for the patio." Then he squinted. "Thought you were sticking with Shirlee."

After I caught my breath, I spread the three pieces of paper on the glass-topped table.

"Evidence," I said. "Had to show you. Right away."

Wil grinned. "So let's have a look at your Mysterious Markings in the Margin." He studied the scrap of paper from the *TV Guide*. "Yup. 'BP' has to be 'Baby Parrots' all right. Ties in with the meeting Friday at twelve."

"And 'Del'? It's 'Deliveries,' right?"

Wil nodded again.

Then I handed him my next piece of evidence—the scribbling from the telephone notepad.

"Now look at this crazy map—or whatever it is," I said. " 'WBX.' 'MALXX.' 'SMX.' And arrows and lines and a big question mark in a circle. What do you think?"

Wil shook his head. "I'm plumb buffaloed."

" 'MALXX' starts out like 'Malibu,' " I said, chewing my thumbnail. "And without the *X*, 'SM' *could* stand for 'Santa Monica.' "

"So what are all the *X*s—"

"Deliveries!" I cried. "That *has* to be it."

"Deliveries of what?"

"Birds, of course."

"So, 'XX,' " I went on, "would be the two deliveries to Malibu that Shirlee talked about—"

"And 'SMX'—that could be the one to Santa Monica," he said.

"Right! Prob'ly Shirlee wrote the question mark because they weren't sure if they should make the Santa Monica delivery Friday or wait until Saturday!"

Wil grinned. "Now we're getting somewhere. But what about 'WBX'?"

I ran my fingers over the paper. "A map, I think. Malibu at the top. Santa Monica at the bottom. And 'WB' in between."

"You mean 'WB' stands for some town?" asked Wil.

I began chewing my thumbnail again. "It should. Except that the only town between Malibu and Santa Monica is Pacific Cliffs."

"Initials P.C.," he said.

"I'm stumped, Wil."

Next I took out the paper from Denise with the semaphore message. "What about this? Can you decode it?"

Wil frowned. "When my little brother was a Cub Scout, we used to practice signal flags. But it's been awhile." He turned the paper around and smiled. "Can't tell which way's up. Too bad you didn't copy the signals, M.D.K. You're an artist. You could draw the flags better."

He studied the paper some more. Finally he nodded. "I

think I remember some of the letters. Got a pencil to write
them down?''

"Darn! I *knew* I should've brought my pack. It's full of
pencils. But tell me the letters.'' I got to my knees. "I'll
scratch them in the sand.''

Wil began, "*T*, blank, blank. . . . Cowboys' bumpers!
I can't remember half of those letters anymore.'' He
scratched his head, then went on. "*Z*, blank, *R*, *O* . . .
blank, *O*, blank, *R*. . . .'' By the time he had finished the
message, there were quite a few blanks. He gave me a
sheepish grin. "Forgot more than I thought.''

I studied the scrapings in the sand: T____ Z__RO
__O__R N__ARS AR__ __O__ R__AD__ OLD
B__DD__. "At least we know it has to do with something old.'' I tried to sound grateful. Wil *had* done his
best.

"Think that last word might be 'bird'?'' he asked. "It
has a *B* and a *D*.''

"No. One too many *D*s, and it's in the wrong place,''
I said. "I wish Denise were here. She may be a klutz, but
she's smart.'' As I scrambled to my feet, I noticed that
something was missing.

"Wil! That tumbler that Denise knocked over yesterday—it's gone. And so's the magazine we left out to dry.''

"Somebody prob'ly walked off with them,'' Wil said.
"Anyone could come onto this patio from the beach.'' He
grinned. "Like me.''

He stuck Denise's notes in his pocket. "I'll keep this.
In case I remember more of the letters.''

I brushed the sand from my knees.

"The library might have a book on semaphore,'' I said.
"I'll check on my way home this afternoon.''

"Even without this, you've got plenty of high-powered
evidence,'' said Wil. "Things don't look as good for ol'

Shirlee and her birdman sweetie as they did. What does your Willy-Nilly man think?''

"Oh, darn!" I rapped my forehead with my knuckles. "I meant to call Mr. Willy-Bones after I talked to you. We've got to find a phone."

Wil glanced toward the sliding glass door of the beach house. "Sure would be handy to call from here. Too bad we can't get in." Then he moved closer to the door. "Did Denise close those curtains when she locked up yesterday?"

"Never noticed," I said. I came closer too, and gave the glass door a slight tug. It slid open!

Wil and I stared at each other.

"Guess Denise didn't lock up after all," I said.

"Maybe she didn't turn the key all the way." Will shrugged. "Or maybe her stepdad got back early."

"*Hope* not," I said.

Wil stepped inside and gestured for me to follow.

"I feel funny going in without Denise," I said.

"Don't reckon she'd mind our making a quick call," Will drawled.

I found the telephone on a stand in the dining area, but no phone book.

"Can't remember Mr. Willy-Bones's number," I said. "I'll have to call information."

There were pencils in a jar next to the phone. I tossed one to Wil. "Use this to write the semaphore letters you figured out."

He took the paper from his pocket, sat down at the dining table, and started writing. An information operator finally gave me the pet shop's number. I jotted it on a scratch pad, then dialed. There was no answer.

"He can't *still* be out buying his lunch," I said, hanging up before the recorded message had a chance to come on. "He must be getting doughnuts for his afternoon snack."

Wil leaped to his feet. "Speaking of chow, how about we amble over to Sam's?"

"Didn't you have lunch yet?"

He nodded. "But that was two hours ago. And I'd like to sample their Tex-Mex—compare it with Shirlee Alabama's."

I tore the top sheet from the scratch pad. "I'll take this number along and try later from a pay phone."

"So do we exit this place by front gate or back?"

"The front door," I said. "The way we came." I was anxious to leave. The house felt strange, different. Was a chair out of place? Something about the curtains?

We stepped onto the sandy patio.

"Shouldn't we lock up?" Will asked.

"We can't without a key."

On the way over to the oyster bar I asked Wil how he had made out with feeding my pets.

He grinned. "A snap!"

Outside Sam's Oyster Bar, Wil grabbed my arm. "The green T-bird—it's heading into the parking lot."

We rushed across the sand. By the time we reached the asphalt parking lot under the pier, Evil Eyes was already gone.

"Let's check out his car," said Wil.

"But what if he sees us?"

"Then you keep watch," said Wil. "I'll check it out alone."

I stood guard a few yards away while Wil walked around the car, looking in the windows and trying the doors.

"Hurry up, Wil." I looked around, feeling more and more scared. "If he catches us—"

A hand clamped my shoulder and yanked me around.

"Wiseacre kid! What're you up to *this* time?"

I stared up at my own reflection—on the shiny black surface of Evil Eyes's sunglasses.

14

A Secret Visitor

LUMP FACE HUNCHED BESIDE EVIL EYES. UP CLOSE he looked even lumpier.

"Wil!" I screamed.

Wil raced over. Evil Eyes let go of my shoulder and turned to scowl at him.

"Whatya doing, messing around my car?" he demanded.

Wil gulped. "Just looking. It's a . . . a real classic."

"I don't like nosy kids messing around my car."

"And we don't like 'em spying on us," Lump Face added with a snarl.

"But we weren't—"

"Shut up, brat." Evil Eyes shook his fist at me, then at Wil. "Clear out—both of you—before I call the cops."

The two men lunged into the green T-bird.

"Wish they *would* call the police," I said as the car roared out of the parking lot. "Or maybe *we* should."

Wil shrugged. "But we don't know if they broke the law."

"Not yet," I said. "But they're planning to."

He shook his head. "According to the law, that's not sufficient evidence."

"Why? We know they're waiting for a delivery of birds," I said.

"They didn't say they were being smuggled—"

"For gosh sakes, Wil! They wouldn't come right out and *say* it. We have to assume—"

"The law won't let you assume. You need proof."

"So what do we do? Trail them, to catch them in the act? We can't do that, Wil. It's too dangerous."

He tugged at his ear. "Wish Dad was here. He'd know what to do."

"Wil, I'm scared."

"It'll be okay." He gave me a comforting smile and started walking. "That ol' guy at the pet shop might have some ideas," he said. "Come on. From Sam's you can phone him."

Following Wil into the Oyster Bar, I felt awful. We were almost positive those two guys were smugglers—and we couldn't do anything about it.

At Sam's we sat at the same table we had eaten at before. Tim took our order. Wil gave him a toothy grin and pointed to the menu.

"A bowl of that Tex-Mex!"

"Sorry," Tim said. "New item. We won't be offering it till this weekend."

Wil looked disappointed. He rubbed his chin. "Then how about . . . a glass of milk? And a hunk of that sourdough bread with butter? But *no* clams."

"Just apple juice for me," I told Tim. "And . . . is there a telephone here?"

"By the door." He pointed. "But it's out of order."

I jumped up. "Forget the apple juice. I'll meet you later, Wil. I'm going back to the beach house to make that call."

Outside I noticed a green car starting down the gravel driveway between the row of beach houses and the highway. The car disappeared before I got a good look at it, but the turquoise green was definitely the shade of Evil Eyes's T-bird. But how could I trail him on foot? I continued along the beach to the patio of the beach house.

Before going in, I shook my sneakers. No sense tracking more sand into the house.

Then it hit me! Today the tile floor was shiny. That's what was different. Yesterday's sandy tracks were gone! And the secret visitor who had swept the floor must have taken away the tumbler and the wildlife magazine, too. But who was it?

Were there more clues inside? As I reached for the door to slide it open, I heard a noise. My hand dropped.

Was someone in the beach house?

15

Where is WB?

I RACED BACK TOWARD SAM'S. THEN I SAW WIL RUNning in my direction, waving his arms.

"M.D.K.!" he shouted. "Guess what?"

"The floor of the house," I cried. "It's *clean*—"

"Tim told me—"

"And I heard—"

"—he knows Evil Eyes—"

"—a noise inside!"

"And he says—"

Face to face by now, we stopped yelling and began to laugh. Then Wil pointed to me. "You first, M.D.K."

When I told him that someone had taken a broom to the tile floor, Wil only shrugged.

"The maid, prob'ly, or a cleaning service. That's who left the door unlocked, I s'pose."

"But I heard a sound, from inside the house."

"Maybe Denise's stepdad really is back."

"She didn't mention it this morning on the phone," I said.

"Wait'll you hear *my* news," Wil said enthusiastically. "I got to talking with our waiter. On a hunch I described Evil Eyes Perry—and Tim knows him!"

"But he told Denise he *didn't*."

93

Wil shook his head. "Didn't know what car the guy drove, that's all. Tim says Perry and his lump-faced friend come to the oyster bar all the time." Wil clamped a hand on my shoulder. "And get this, M.D.K.! They're friends with Denise's stepdad *and* a bunch of old ex-surfers who hang around the pier."

"Like the Old Geezer?" I asked.

"And maybe the Parrot Man, too."

I started up the incline from the beach. "We've got to find a phone. I must tell Mr. Willy-Bones about Evil Eyes."

"Tim says the nearest pay phone is across the highway."

We hurried to the crosswalk, and as soon as the light turned green, we dashed across Pacific Coast Highway to the phone. Between us we dug up enough dimes to call Pacific Cliffs.

"Read me the number while I dial," I said as I handed Wil the paper I'd torn from the notepad at the beach house.

He frowned. "Why'd you write it twice?"

"But I *didn't*." I stared at the two numbers—the second in someone's else's handwriting. "It must have been there already. I never noticed."

"Who else would want to call the pet shop?" Wil asked.

"Not Denise. Until I introduced them, she didn't even know Mr. Willy-Bones. And she told me Floyd didn't know him either."

Then I gasped. "Only one person up here knows Mr. Willy-Bones. Evil Eyes Perry! Remember? He even said he'd phone the pet shop when he had some birds to sell."

Wil scowled. "What would ol' Evil Eyes be doing in the beach house?"

"He knows Floyd. Tim said so. That means he knows that Floyd's gone . . . and the beach house is empty," I said. "What better place for Evil Eyes to run his smuggling operation?"

Wil shook his head. "Pretty far-out theory, M.D.K."

"There's something else I forgot to tell you. After leaving Sam's, I saw a green car on the road behind Denise's beach house. I'm almost positive it was—"

"Hey, girlie?" A gum-chewing surfer leaning against his upright board glared at me. "You gonna make a phone call or what?"

Flustered, I dropped in the coins and dialed while Wil read me the number.

Again no answer, and after three rings the answering machine. This time I had to take a chance. I waited for the beep and began babbling—about Evil Eyes and deliveries and the Fish and Wildlife people. In the middle of it all a second beep sounded. My time was up.

We left the phone to the sullen surfer and crossed the highway.

"I'm not even sure what I said," I told Wil. "Or if it made sense. Or if I told all I meant to. I *hate* talking to answering machines."

Wil grinned. "Never talked to one."

By now the sun was low over the ocean. Cars were pulling out of the parking lots, and the beach crowd was thinning. Only a handful of determined fishermen still dangled their lines off Malibu Pier.

"Must be after five," I said. "I've got to be getting home."

Wil nodded. "Tomorrow's Friday—the big day," he said. "We should meet early, in case the boat Evil Eyes is meeting arrives at noon."

"And if it doesn't?"

"We'll just have to camp out till midnight."

"I don't care if Shirlee *does* object," I said. "I'll be there!"

While waiting for the bus, Wil handed me the semaphore notes. ''You'll need them to look up the signals at the library.''

On the ride back to Pacific Cliffs, I puzzled over Shirlee's doodling. ''If the Xs stand for deliveries of baby parrots . . . then that 'WBX' must mean one delivery at 'WB'—''

''Whatever town that is.''

I drew in my breath. ''Oh, Wil—'WB' is not a *town*.''

''What is it?'' He started to grin. ''Whale Barnacles?''

''No,'' I said. ''It's Mr. Willy-Bones, otherwise known as Wilhelm Bjornson!''

16

The Zero Hour

I STEPPED THROUGH THE FRONT DOORWAY AND sniffed. Fried chicken! That was a switch! Why? I wondered. What happened to all those jars of chili?

Shirlee got up from the E-Z lounger and switched off the television. "Thought you were goin' to stay home all day today, Miss Margaret."

"Changed my mind," I said.

She looked down her thin nose at me. "So where have you been?"

"Out."

Shirlee eyed me suspiciously. "Not gallivantin' after lawbreakers, tryin' to be a hero, are you?"

"Me? Why would I do a silly thing like that?"

"Hmph," she snorted. "Not silly—dangerous!"

She stomped into the kitchen. I followed, trying to convince myself she was no criminal, but only my well-meaning, nosy sitter.

During dinner I had no chance to ask what *she* had done all day. She began asking more questions as soon as we sat down. It was like being on trial.

"Did you go up to Malibu again?" Shirlee demanded.

Did she know? I stared at her, then nodded. "For a little while. . . . Wil wanted to . . . go surfing."

97

So it was stretching the truth. But Wil *might* have gone surfing, if we hadn't been trailing our suspects.

Her eyes narrowed. "You didn't talk to strangers?"

"Of course not."

"You're sure?"

The way she said that so quickly, I could tell—she *did* know! I drew back. "Well, I . . . talked to the bus driver . . . and to people fishing on the pier." That was true, anyway.

After I finished eating, I jumped up from the table.

"Why don't you go watch TV?" I said. "I'll do the dishes tonight."

Her red eyebrows arched, then she smiled. "Why, thank you, Miss Margaret. I *am* tired—it's been a busy week."

I'll bet!

But instead of settling in front of the TV, Shirlee headed for the den.

"Going to bed this early?" I asked.

She gave me a tight-lipped smile. "A busy day tomorrow."

Her door closed. I had no chance to ask, "Doing what?"

It didn't matter. I already knew. She and Jerome had those two deliveries to make in Malibu, and the one delivery here in town to 'WB'—Wilhelm Bjornson. But deliveries of what, I didn't want to know.

While loading the dishwasher, I thought about Mr. Willy-Bones. Even though he seemed to know Shirlee, I still couldn't believe he was plotting and planning with the smugglers.

Maybe I should try one more time to call him.

But before I got the chance, the phone rang.

I grabbed it on the first ring. It was Denise. Since Shirlee didn't come running, she must be asleep already.

"Did you get the semaphore message to Wil?" Denise asked. "Was it important?"

"We figured out part of it and hoped you could unravel the rest. But how can you by phone?"

"I will copy it and have a try," Denise said. "Should be a cinch, if you have watched as many episodes of *Wheel of Fortune* as I have."

Pulling out the paper, I read the letters and the blanks to her.

"Simple!" she said. "You start with vowels." There was a pause. "I'm not sure about the first word. But obviously the next one, *Z*, blank, *R*, *O*, is 'zero.'" Another pause. "*N*, blank, *A*, *R*, *S*, is 'nears,' of course. And the last word—"

"Wil suggested 'bird,'" I said, trying to be helpful.

"Ridiculous. 'Bird' has only one *D*. Undoubtedly it ends in a *Y*. But I don't know what the vowel is after *B*. So the word is either 'baddy' or 'beddy' or 'biddy'—"

I rubbed my forehead as I tried to think. "Shirlee is Jerome's girlfriend, so he wouldn't call her an old biddy."

"I have it!" shouted Denise. "It is 'buddy.' He called the Geezer 'old buddy.'"

Knowing the signs for *E*, *U*, and *Y* made it easy for us to figure out more words. As Denise and I worked together, I scribbled in the letters. Then I read from my scribbling.

"Listen to this," I said. "'The zero' . . . something . . . 'nears. Are you ready, old buddy?'"

"Obviously 'zero *hour*,'" Denise cried. "The hour at which a previously planned operation takes place."

"Meaning the arrival tomorrow at twelve of the smuggled birds," I announced triumphantly.

Now for sure it seemed that the Parrot Man and the Old Geezer were on the side of Evil Eyes and his fellow smugglers. But what about Shirlee?

"Incidentally, after my optometrist's appointment I checked Jerome's mailbox," Denise said. "Thought there might be another letter from Brazil."

"Denise! Tampering with the U.S. mail is a federal offense."

"I didn't tamper. I looked," she said. "But the box merely contained another reminder about that Old-Timer Lifeguards' beach party on Friday at Malibu. 'Food, fun, frolic with friends.' Sounds ghastly."

"Just so they don't get in our way when we track down the smugglers," I said.

"What is tomorrow's schedule?" she asked.

"We meet Wil on the bus that gets here at nine," I said. "So we have to take care of the pets really early."

"Would it help if I assist with the birds after I tend Hilda and Conrad?"

"It would!" I said. "Oh, and I almost forgot—I discovered when I took your notes up to Wil in Malibu that someone broke into your beach house last night."

"Was a window smashed?"

"No! No broken locks, either. It was really mysterious."

"You are positive someone broke in?"

I recounted the clues: the swept floor, the pet shop's telephone number on the notepad, and the unlocked door.

"Oh my gosh," said Denise. "Floyd will have a *fit*."

"When will he be back?"

"This weekend sometime."

"He's in for a surprise," I said. "My theory is that Evil Eyes uses your place as a headquarters for his smuggling operation."

"M.D.K., that is absurd!"

"I know," I said. "But what other explanation is there?"

Suddenly I heard Shirlee's door open. As she padded into the kitchen, I slammed down the phone.

"Couldn't sleep," Shirlee said. "Too much on my mind. Think I'll make myself a cup of cocoa. Want me to make some for you, too, sweetie?"

"No, thanks."

I went to my room and flopped onto the bed.

But before switching off my light, I opened my sketchbook and flipped past the lists of clues and evidence. On a blank page, I printed in huge purple letters: AT LAST, THE ZERO HOUR!

17

Lookout for Smugglers

IT WAS STILL DARK WHEN MY ALARM WENT OFF. I dragged myself out of bed. The sound of muffled voices came from the kitchen. Was it burglars? I panicked. Should I stay in my room, or make a run for the front door? Then Shirlee's familiar cackle calmed me. There was nothing to fear.

Or was there? I kept forgetting that I was sharing the house with a smuggler's moll capable of almost anything! And for Shirlee to be up this early was highly suspicious.

Quickly I put on my purple T-shirt and white shorts—fresh from the dryer. Yuck! Shirlee had even *ironed* the shorts. Oh well—I guess she was only trying to be nice. But . . . would a member of a smuggler's gang do that? Maybe we were wrong about her. Or was this a trick of Shirlee's to throw me off?

I pulled on my sneakers, grabbed my pack, and rushed into the hall. On hearing a man's voice, I skidded to a stop.

"Mrs. Alabama, does this go too?" I recognized the voice. The Parrot Man!

"You bet!" said Shirlee. "Put it in that box over there."

Put *what* in a box? Were they stealing Mom's silverware? I ran back to my room. Now what? Those two mustn't see me leave. Luckily Mom had left the screen off my window, for quick escape in case of emergency. And this was an emergency!

I tossed my pack, then jumped. Was I glad we didn't have a two-story house. But as I dashed across the front yard, Shirlee and Jerome came out of the house, carrying two big cardboard cartons. I ducked behind a thick eugenia bush. They mustn't find out I was on my way to Malibu.

Parked at the curb was a battered blue van. Why was it here? What were they up to?

I watched them load the boxes into the van. At least they weren't stealing Mom's silver. She didn't own that much. They brought out two more boxes. What was in them? As soon as Shirlee and Jerome again disappeared into the house, I rushed to the van and peered in.

"Away!" squawked the red parrot from inside the van. *"Go away!"*

Jerome came running. I fled down the street without looking back. Had he seen me or not? Long after the sound of Casper's screeching had died, I kept running. My heart still pounded when I got to Bun's yard. But by the time I fed him and left, I had calmed down.

On the way to feed the tortoise, I met Denise. She was carrying a blanket and a big beach bag.

"Rising at dawn is *so invigorating*." She fluffed her hair. "I even had time to play with Izzy. I decided to keep her—no matter what Floyd says."

While scattering lettuce for the tortoise, I told Denise about the van and the cartons Shirlee and Jerome were loading.

"Possibly containers for transporting smuggled birds."

"But if the boxes were empty, why carry them so carefully?"

Denise rolled her eyes, gazing upward as if in a trance.

"In time the answer will reveal itself." Then she grinned. "How ironic. A week ago I never *dreamed* we would be friends and I would be assisting in the apprehension of underworld malefactors."

"I guess," I said, not sure what she meant. "But how strange—it was all because of that red macaw. When he ruined Hilda's leash, I needed money quick and went looking for clients in Edgecliff Estates. . . . You saw me . . . we became partners . . . you saw that reward notice—"

"Rather like that old saying: 'For want of a nail the shoe was lost, for want of a shoe the horse was lost—' "

"Never mind." I couldn't see what horses had to do with parrots. "Your bag looks heavy. What's in it?"

"Books, Floyd's binoculars . . . and sufficient sustenance to last until midnight—if necessary."

"Let's hope it isn't."

We fed the canaries and rushed for the bus, getting to the stop as the bus eased to the curb. Wil sat up front. I flopped beside him and rested my pack on my knees. Denise settled into the seat behind us.

We were quiet once I'd filled Wil in on the strange activities of Shirlee and Jerome. Halfway to Malibu I suddenly thought: What if the smugglers never showed up? I turned to Wil. "This *could* turn out to be a wild goose chase."

"Wild parrot chase, you mean." He grinned.

"What if Mr. Willy-Bones never got my message? What if he never called the Fish and Wildlife agents?"

"Don't worry," Wil said. "I'll bet the pier is already swarming with undercover agents."

"How do we recognize them?"

"Prob'ly won't," drawled Wil. "Otherwise they wouldn't be undercover, would they?"

As soon as we got off the bus, we hurried across the Coast Highway.

"Let's set up our command post close enough to the pier so we can spot the boat when it arrives," Wil said.

"Sorry I cannot let you use the beach house," Denise said. "But my mother forbade me to go near it. She is coming up this afternoon to discuss the break-in with the authorities."

After some searching, we found a deserted stretch of beach south of the pier, halfway between the beach house and the water's edge.

"Perfect," said Wil. "And we've also got a good view of Sam's and the parking lot."

"And of the beach house, too—in case it's the hideout of Evil Eyes." When I said that, they both gave me weird looks.

We dubbed our location Station One. Denise spread the blanket on the sand and brought out potato chips and lemonade.

"Two of us at a time can go on patrol," Wil said between gulps of lemonade. "Whoever's at Station One can survey the whole area."

"What if there's an emergency?" I asked.

"The person at Station One can wave a blanket," Denise said. "And since we patrol in pairs, one of the two can run back."

"Right." I crunched a potato chip. If things got desperate, would I still remember all those rules?

Wil looked thoughtful. "Prob'ly the smugglers will dock at the end of the pier in one of those fishing boats."

He and Denise took the first patrol. As they started off, Wil pointed. A boat plowed toward the pier, a flock of hungry gulls circling overhead.

"This could be it," he yelled to Denise, and off they went.

Soon they were back.

"False alarm," Wil told me. "Denise and I'll check Sam's and the parking lot. Keep your eyes peeled for smugglers."

I scanned the beach crowd. It was like when I fly with Mom and we scan the skies for traffic. Only this time I was looking for Evil Eyes and his gang. I didn't see them anywhere.

By noon we'd raced to the pier a dozen times to check out fishing boats. All were just that: fishing boats. By then we had finished all the lemonade and chips and most of the apples and muffins Denise had brought. I dug into my pack.

"Time out for emergency-supply trail mix," I said.

After that Wil and I went on patrol. That's when we saw the blue van. It was in the parking lot, and unloading cartons from it were Jerome and the Old Geezer.

"The Loathsome Twosome!" shouted Wil.

I peered through the binoculars Denise had lent me. "Should we close in?"

"First let's see what they're up to. . . . Maybe they'll make contact with Evil Eyes."

I scanned the crowd with Floyd's heavy binoculars. A bag lady in a striped stocking cap pulled in a fish, but there was no sign of Evil Eyes.

Next I checked the ocean. Beyond a string of small sailboats with brilliant spinnakers, two power boats zoomed toward shore. Gulls circled above one of them, which probably meant it was a fishing boat with a good catch.

Suddenly Wil shouted. "Jerome is heading for the beach. The Geezer, too. I'll trail them."

"Wait!" I shouted. "I may have spotted—" But already Wil was loping across the sand.

18

Trapped!

I COULDN'T FOLLOW WIL. MY LEGS WEREN'T NEARLY as long as his. I'd never catch up. Should I alert Denise? No. I'd stay here to find where those power boats were headed.

Near shore they separated. One nosed toward the pier. The other turned south.

Clutching the binoculars, I ran up the incline next to Sam's Oyster Bar. That fishing boat would dock soon. Were the smugglers aboard? I had to warn the Fish and Wildlife agents.

Sneakers thumping, I raced along the wooden pier. Visible through cracks in the boards, the surf roared onto the sandy shore, then surged back again. Farther out, beyond the breakers, the blue-green ocean lay beneath me. It was a long way down. I grew dizzy.

At the end of the pier, past the sightseers and people fishing, I stopped. What now? Who in that mob were undercover agents? I couldn't very well call out, "Hey, agents!"

Feeling like a real dork, I turned around and ran back along the creaky pier to Sam's. I scooted down the sandy incline onto the crowded beach. Glancing toward the parking lot, I spotted Evil Eyes. He was climbing into his car.

Then the green Thunderbird roared from the lot, pulled onto Pacific Coast Highway, and headed south.

He was taking a load of smuggled birds to the pet shop in Pacific Cliffs—that *had* to be it! We were too late. The smugglers had slipped past us.

Now it was Mr. Willy-Bones I had to warn. I raced to the beach house to phone him. Even if it was Evil Eyes's hangout, he was gone. It was safe now.

I pushed the sliding door at the front. It wouldn't budge. Had Evil Eyes locked it? But that was impossible. He'd need a key.

I crept around through the shortcut at the side of the house to check the back door. It was unlocked. What luck! I slipped inside and tiptoed through the kitchen and into the dining area. Then I stopped. In the living room people were talking.

But who? Evil Eyes was on his way to Pacific Cliffs. I crouched behind the counter to listen.

". . . so first thing tomorrow we'll come by." The man spoke with a deep, husky voice. There was a pause. Then he said, "Right. . . . With the birds. . . . See you then. . . ."

It wasn't two people. It was one man, talking on the telephone. I recognized the rumbly voice. It was Lump Face!

I backed into the kitchen, darted out the back door, and raced for the garage. That was the quickest way out.

Before my hand touched the doorknob, it began to turn. Someone was coming in through the garage.

I ran to the side yard and pulled the gate closed behind me. Then I stood motionless.

The door to the garage squeaked open, then slammed shut. All was quiet. Then feet thumped on a step. Paper rustled—a grocery bag, maybe? A door opened and closed.

Whoever it was had gone in the back door. He—or she—was now in the beach house. Trying to escape through the front patio was risky. The garage was still the way to go.

But when I tried the door, it was locked.

I dashed to the side yard again, then crept through the shortcut to the front. Before pushing open the gate, I had to make sure no one was in the patio.

The gate was a foot higher than the top of my head. I looked around for something to stand on. I spotted a small corrugated-cardboard box. That might work. After dumping out the weeds, I turned the box over and stepped on it gingerly. Then I peeked over the top of the gate.

Horrors! Lump Face and Evil Eyes were sitting in the patio.

I was trapped!

19

A Prisoner

I HOPPED OFF THE BOX AND HUDDLED ON THE BRICK path, hugging my knees. What now? I was right about Evil Eyes. He *had* taken over the beach house for his hangout. But being right didn't solve my problem. How was I going to get away from here?

The garage was locked. The fences around the beach house were much too high to climb. As for leaving through the front patio, forget it! Those two were *smugglers*! If they found I was spying, they'd be furious. No telling what they'd do to me.

What I needed was my pack. It contained things I could use right now, like a bandanna to wave for a signal to Wil and Denise, or paper to fold into an airplane so I could sail an SOS message over the neighbor's fence. My Swiss Army knife would be the most useful of all right now. I could pick the lock in the garage door. I could even make a run for it. With my knife I could defend myself as I raced past those two.

Was there anything useful in the trash from that box? As I sifted through the weeds in it, I found a yellow-green feather. But this downy-soft feather was not from a gull! It must have come from a baby parrot!

This was my proof that there *was* a smuggling operation. And this beach house was its headquarters.

But being right didn't help much this time either. I was still a prisoner.

"Hey, Ernie?" It was Lump Face's gravelly voice.

Were they about to make plans? I jumped back on my box to eavesdrop. The two men wouldn't notice. They had their backs to me.

"I told you to get grape," Lump Face grumbled. "Didn't the 7-Eleven have any grape?"

"Yeah, they had grape."

"Then how come you didn't get any?"

"Eat your orange Popsicle and stop complaining. . . ."

They weren't making plans. Evil Eyes hadn't delivered smuggled birds to Mr. Willy-Bones. He had gone to the 7-Eleven for Popsicles!

Was I wrong about the feather?

"But I don't *like* orange. . . ." Lump Face was still grousing.

I licked my dry lips. A cold, sweet, sticky, juicy Popsicle—any flavor—would taste so good that I tried not to think about it. I was so hot and thirsty, I was ready to faint.

"How come you didn't get grape, Ernie?"

" 'Cause Floyd only likes orange. So knock it off, willya?"

Floyd? Then it wasn't a break-in. Floyd knew they were there. But if he was back from his fishing trip, where was he?

"All I'm sayin' is *next* time—"

"*Shut up!* I'm trying to concentrate on what I'm doin'."

Evil Eyes had finished his Popsicle. He was scanning the beach with binoculars.

"Whatya see?" Lump Face asked.

Evil Eyes mumbled something I didn't hear.

Whatever he was looking at, I wanted to see it too. I lifted the binoculars hanging from my neck and rested them on the top of the gate.

I scanned the beach. The Parrot Man waved semaphore flags. At first I thought he was signaling the two men at the beach house. But Evil Eyes paid no attention. I looked more to the left. On a bluff the Old Geezer stood, waving his flags.

"So whatya see?" Lump Face asked again.

"Boat's at anchor . . . the dinghy's heading for shore."

What boat? The smugglers'? Ignoring the Parrot Man, I scanned farther out. I couldn't locate the boat they talked about. But I saw the dinghy, bobbing and tipping in the surf. Three men were trying to drag it onto the beach.

"Floyd's havin' a little trouble," said Evil Eyes.

Floyd? Was he one of the *smugglers*? How awful! How would I ever tell Denise?

"The dinghy's tipping!" cried Evil Eyes.

"Lemme see!" Lump Face snatched the binoculars.

Elbowing him away, Evil Eyes grabbed them back.

While they fought over the binoculars, I watched the little boat. A huge wave scooped it up and flipped it over. Around it the surf was dotted with orange blobs. What were they?

Waist-deep in water, the men floundered, grabbing for the blobs.

"The jackets! They got dumped out!" yelled Evil Eyes.

"Think we oughta go help 'em?"

Why all the excitement? Those men wouldn't drown. They were *already* wearing life vests. Why did they need more?

Suddenly my cardboard box began to sag. With both hands, I grabbed the gate top.

"*Yikes!*" I cried as the gate swung out, taking me with it.

I dropped onto the sandy patio floor. Before I could scramble to my feet, Evil Eyes grabbed my shoulder.

"It's the wiseacre kid!" Evil Eyes snarled. "What're you doin' here?"

"Nothing. Let me *go*!" I tried to break free. "I didn't do anything. . . . "

"You been spyin' on me." Gritting his ugly yellow teeth, Evil Eyes leaned over until his face was close to mine. "Whatya think, I'm stupid or something? I saw you and your little friends up on the pier."

"But we *weren't* spying." I began to cry.

"Gimme the binoculars, Ernie. I want to see how Floyd's doing."

Evil Eyes didn't give them up. "No. You take care of our wiseacre friend," he said, running from the patio. "I'm going down to help."

Lump Face locked pudgy hands on both my shoulders and called after him. "Whatya want me to do with her?"

"Lock her in the closet," Evil Eyes shouted, "—for now."

20

Contraband

"GET MOVING."

When Lump Face ordered me into the house, I dug my heels into the sand. He struggled to drag me in.

Suddenly I screamed. "Behind you! *Look out!*"

The oldest trick in the book—but the lunk fell for it. He turned around. His grip loosened. I squirmed free and ran across the patio. Then I whirled to face him.

"You want binoculars? *Here! Take these!*"

Yanking Floyd's heavy binoculars from my neck, I swung them by the strap and let go. They struck his shoulder. Lump Face reeled back, and I sprinted.

The Old Geezer was just ahead. I wasn't sure I could trust him. But I had no choice.

"Help!" I shouted, pointing back at Lump Face, who was chasing me. "He's a smuggler. And those guys . . ." I waved toward the beach. ". . . in life vests . . . smugglers too . . . baby parrots . . ."

The Geezer flipped his two flags for a couple of seconds. Then he charged at Lump Face. For an old guy, he was fast—and strong. He planted a fist in the lunk's doughy stomach. Lump Face went down, and when he scrambled to his feet, the Geezer came at him again. He raced for the beach house, the Geezer on his heels.

114

I headed for the men from the dinghy. Evil Eyes was with them now. They staggered up the sloping beach. Their wet pants and shirts stuck to them. Each man wore a life jacket and clutched two or more. What was in those jackets?

"M.D.K.!"

I turned. Wil ploughed toward me through the soft sand.

"Where you been?" he called. "We searched *everywhere*!"

"Long story . . . come on." I broke into a run.

Wil jogged beside me. "But Denise is looking for you. . . . We should tell her—"

"No time. . . . Those guys . . . with the orange vests. They're smugglers."

"You're sure?"

"Positive. . . . No time to explain. . . . Trust me." In the dry sand my feet sank. It was like running through molasses.

"Cowboys' bumpers! Ol' Floyd's with them."

"He's part of the gang. . . . So is Evil Eyes."

When we got closer to the men, I began to shout. "We know what you are!"

The walked faster.

"Everybody knows!" I yelled. "We've caught you—"

"Get lost," one of them yelled. All the men began to run. They split up.

"We'd better split up too," said Wil. He zoomed off.

"Yahoo!" The loud Texas shout echoed down the beach. Wil leaped over a kid's sand castle and tackled Evil Eyes.

I chased a short, fat man—the slowest of the group. He zigzagged around the kids playing ball. Closing in, I snatched at one of the vests the man carried.

"Get lost, punk!" he shouted.

"No way!" I yelled at him. "We'll tell the FBI . . . the lifeguards . . . the police."

He glowered down at me. "I said beat it, kid."

People glanced up from their sunbathing and card playing.

I screamed even louder. "We've called the Fish and Wildlife people. . . . They're here. . . . You're smugglers, and *we've caught you*!"

Now sunbathers and card players leaped up and formed a semicircle around the man and me. He tried to slink away, but I snatched at one of the life jackets he was carrying.

He snarled and backed off. "Brat! Leave that alone."

I grabbed again. The man twisted away, dropping the orange vest on the sand.

I reached for it.

"Give that *back*!" he shouted.

I took off, but my feet sank deep into the dry sand. I tried to go faster as the man started after me. But I couldn't. Then two surfers lunged at him, knocked him to the ground, and sat on him. A lifeguard raced over, blowing his whistle.

Jerome ran past, the squawking parrot perched on his shoulder and three lifeguards running beside him.

"The guys . . . with the life jackets!" I yelled. "They're bird smugglers."

The guards and Jerome ran on. But I couldn't go another step. Panting, I flopped onto the beach with the orange vest.

"M.D.K.!" Denise stood over me. "Where have you *been*? We thought you were *kidnapped*."

I sat up. "Almost was—by the smugglers."

She looked back toward the pier. "But we were watching—"

"The smugglers landed on the beach."

A lifeguard truck sped by on the hard, wet sand at the water's edge. Another followed close behind. From the other direction rolled another official-looking car. Its siren wailed.

"Come on, M.D.K.!" Denise yelled. "We have to help."

"Hold it," I shouted. She stopped, then dragged back. "They only had two left to catch." I didn't add that Floyd was one of them. "By now they must have them all."

Denise stood drooping on the sand. "Apprehended already. And I missed it all."

"Maybe not *all*." I pointed to the life vest in her hands.

"Feels lumpy," Denise said, patting it.

Then she gasped. "Listen! Hear that?" From under the jacket's orange nylon cover came a faint bleating sound like a baby lamb.

"Denise," I said. "There's a *bird* in there."

Two Mysteries Solved

WE HAD NO TROUBLE FINDING A FISH AND WILDLIFE agent to give the orange life jacket to. By now uniformed officers seemed to be everywhere.

Afterward Denise and I sat for a long time, talking. I told her what had happened at the beach house, and about the feather, and as much as I knew about Floyd. She cried when she found out.

"I'm really sorry, Denise. Even if he was a crim—I mean, even if he broke the law, he *was* your—"

She broke in. "That's okay. It was just a shock. . . . That is all." She got to her feet. "I think I had better phone my mother." She managed a half smile. "M.D.K., if I go up to Oregon to stay with my dad for a while . . . would you look after Isadora for me?"

I nodded. "Sure. What's one more pet?"

Denise's mother was already at the beach house when we got there. As I left them, to head down the beach to look for Wil, I turned to wave to Denise. "See you soon, partner."

She grinned and waved back. "You bet!"

By now sunbathers had returned to sunbathing, card players to card playing. Kids were again building sand castles. Music from transistor radios and the sweet smell of coconut suntan oil filled the air. Frisbee games started up again.

I met a Fish and Wildlife agent carrying one of the orange life jackets.

"Will the baby birds be okay?" I asked.

She smiled. "Those I've seen so far are just fine. They're luckier than most. As far as we can tell, they're just scared—and terribly dehydrated. They'll be all right, I think. We'll get them to an animal hospital right away."

"Then what happens to them?"

"Those that survive both the stress of their illegal entry *and* the rigors of quarantine will be sold at auction. Run by the U.S.D.A."

I looked up, puzzled.

"U.S. Department of Agriculture," she explained.

"I hope someone nice buys them," I told her.

"Maybe you will—with your reward money."

I gasped. I'd forgotten the reward. The five hundred dollars was ours. Wow!

Then I shook my head. "I almost bought a parakeet. But I've been thinking about birds and cages. I want my parakeet to live in a bird zoo."

She nodded. "In a cage so big he won't know it's there, right?"

I grinned. "Right!"

Wil stood at the water's edge, watching surfers help lifeguards beach Floyd's blue-rubber dinghy.

"That was a surprise about ol' Floyd," Wil said.

"I was just thinking about all those life jackets in his garage," I said. "I wondered why those brand-new ones were ripped up. Now it makes sense."

Wil nodded. "And when Tim told me about Floyd and Evil Eyes being buddies, I had a hunch there was more to his trips to Mexico than catching fish."

I smiled at Wil. "Should've followed through on that hunch."

We walked behind three Fish and Wildlife agents who were moving up the beach toward the pier. I pointed to a grungy character joking with them.

"See that bag lady in the striped stocking cap?" I whispered to Wil. "I saw her earlier, fishing from the pier."

"Undercover agent, prob'ly," Wil said.

"So I finally found out what they look like."

Wil stopped and sniffed. "With all that's happened, I must be getting delirious," he said. " 'Cause I swear—I smell chili."

I pointed ahead to where a cluster of old people surrounded Shirlee Alabama. "I'll bet what she's heating over my dad's camp stove is her world-famous Tex-Mex."

"Why would she do that?"

"Because I *think* this is the Old-Timer Lifeguard Association get-together," I said, grinning at Wil. "Remember that postcard in Jerome's trash?"

Wil slapped his thigh. "Detective Kincaid, you did it again."

"Hey!" he added. "That must be what the semaphore message was about. Maybe the Geezer's an ex-lifeguard too."

"And that's why Shirlee made all the chili, I'll bet. Then she and Jerome hauled it to the beach party in those cardboard cartons—" Suddenly I shrieked. "*Beach party!* That's it, Wil. That's the 'BP' in the note!"

Shirlee looked up. She gave a cackly laugh when she saw us.

"What're you-all doin' here at the beach?"

Wil grinned. "We thought we might do a little surfing." He winked at me.

"Long as you're here," Shirlee said, "get in line. . . .

Join the party. Did you catch the excitement down the way?''

We nodded and tried to look nonchalant.

Dad's little propane camp stove couldn't begin to keep that huge pot of Tex-Mex hot. But I was so hungry, and Shirlee's chili was so hot with spices, that even stone cold it tasted good.

"What's the occasion, ma'am?" Wil asked after we gobbled down the chili and were returning the bowls.

Shirlee pressed her thin lips in a smile. "Get-together of all the old lifeguards who worked this beach. My friend Jerome used to be a lifeguard, you know."

I looked at her. "Why didn't you tell me why you were cooking so much chili?"

"You never asked," she said.

"That's a lot of work, ma'am," said Wil. "To feed a mob this size."

"It's my new business," Shirlee told him, her pointy chin jutting out proudly. "A caterin' service. . . . Didn't want to tell your daddy till I was sure how it'd work out. But it's doin' just fine." She looked around and beamed. "Why, I've lined up customers from Santa Monica to Malibu—"

I broke in. "Like maybe Mr. Willy-Bones?"

"That's nice Swedish fella?" Shirlee nodded. "Him too. Why *ever'body* seems to like my Tex-Mex. Including my new partner." She fluttered her lashes at Jerome, standing nearby. "So I guess I'm in California to stay."

From the pocket of her jeans she took two business cards and handed them to Wil and me. The cards had red-checkered borders and said SHIRLEE'S TEX-MEX. SURELY THE BEST IN THE WEST.

Shirlee's famous Tex-Mex recipe

1/8 lb. finely chopped suet*
3 lbs. Round Steak, cut up
6 Tbsp. chili powder
1 Tbsp. ground oregano
1 Tbsp. crushed cumin seed
1 Tbsp. salt
1/2 to 1 Tbsp. cayenne pepper
2 large garlic cloves, chopped
1 Tbsp. hot pepper sauce—"if you dare!"
1 1/2 quarts water
1/2 cup white corn meal *or* 3 Tbsp. masa harina

Fry suet until crisp—add meat & brown. Add seasonings, water & boil. Simmer 1 1/2 hrs. Cool & skim fat. Stir in cornmeal. Simmer 30 minutes. Serve with corn bread and gallons of iced tea!

3–4 Tbsp. of Crisco or cooking oil may be used instead

About the Author

Kathy Pelta is an artist, writer, journalist, and pilot. She has written a number of fiction and nonfiction books for children, including *The Blue Empress*, to which *The Parrot Man Mystery* is a sequel. Ms. Pelta lives in the San Francisco Bay Area with her husband.